BOATS, BUNNIES, AND BODIES

A MOLLY BREWSTER MYSTERY

PAM MOLL

BEAU RIDGE PUBLISHING

Boats, Bunnies and Bodies

Holidays are Murder Series
A Molly Brewster Mystery with Killer Recipes

A Novel by Pam Moll
Copyright ©2019 by Pamela Laux Moll
First paperback edition © December 2019
by Pam Moll
Printed in the United States of America
www.gopamela.com
ISBN: 978-1-892357-09-0
Beau Ridge Publishing

HOLIDAYS ARE MURDER SERIES:

A Molly Brewster Cozy Mystery
with Killer Recipes

Peppermint Mocha Murder
Boats, Bunnies and Bodies
The Fourth Murder
Turkey, Dressing, and the Departed
Champagne, Confetti and a Corpse
Mother's Day, Mayhem and Murder
Pumpkin Covered Corpse
Gingerbread and Dead

NOTE FROM THE AUTHOR

If you've never read a Molly Brewster mystery, you can start with Peppermint Mocha Murder, the first book in the cozy murder mystery series. If you prefer to start with this book, here are a few characters and things you need to know.

Molly "Mo" Brewster — owns *Addicted to the Bean,* a café in the small town of Bay Isles, Florida
Deputy Drew "Lucky" Powell – Palma County Sheriff
Granny Dee McFadden – Mo's cankerous grandmother
Snickers – Molly's Chocolate Lab sidekick
Kona - her adopted Siamese cat
Nadine McFadden Brewster – Molly's usually absent mother
Mayor Clawson - Mayor of Bay Isles
Todd Clawson - the Mayor's son
Aurora Kelly – Barista at the Bean, Molly's best friend
Bailey (Bales) Smith – Barista at the Bean
Henrietta Filadora – Granny Dee's cook
Jet Mitterhammer – Granny's Gardener
Timothy Carlin - Granny's sometimes suitor
Christine - the police station dispatcher

A thief is a thief, whether he steals a boat or a chocolate chip cookie.

CHAPTER ONE

The air inside my cramped costume felt stifling hot. Instead of being at my café and sinking my teeth into a warm blueberry muffin, I was sweating it out at the park. My legs stuck to the polyester-lined suit, making a swooshing sound every time I walked.

Usually, I loved a Florida park on a spring day. Today the sky was a Tiffany blue, waves of wildflowers bloomed, and I wore a furry lime green bunny suit. On the outside, I looked like a giant Easter Bunny. On the inside, I was a sweaty, hot mess.

My once-tamed red hair was twisted in frizzy tufts plastered to my scalp. The fake-fur costume in 80-degree weather had succeeded in raising my body temperature so much that I sweated like an ice-cold glass of caramel Frappuccino.

"I can't believe you talked me into this," I whispered to Aurora, trying to maneuver my fingers free from the mitten paws.

"You're doing great, Mo," Aurora encouraged. "Your tail wiggles when you walk." She suppressed a laugh.

From what I could see through the slits in the giant bunny head, Aurora wore her auburn hair in her signature spiked bob.

A brown tortoiseshell-colored comb with rhinestones held one side behind her right ear.

Since she had started dating the mayor's son, Todd, I had noticed a slight change in her appearance, like using less mousse in her hair and fewer earrings in her ears.

"I'm just saying, if I ever dreamed of dressing up like a bunny, which I haven't, I'm pretty sure it would be that pink number Paris Hilton wore to the Playboy mansion. This is not my idea of a fun costume." I rolled my eyes. Not that she could see my green orbs through the small openings.

We were at the base of the giant flagpole in Fort DeSoto Park, within our little village of Bay Isles. The park, located at the southern tip of our island, consisted of mostly beaches and camping grounds. The historical fort in the middle of the park was built during the Spanish-American War to protect the entrance to Tampa Bay.

The fort was abandoned after WWII to become a county park. The park's most recent claim to fame was from the movie *Magic Mike* and the scene where Mike and Adam worked off excess energy by jumping off the Fort DeSoto bridge. The actor Channing Tatum and his crew's glistening pecs and glutes were exotic dancing all over Bay Isles.

Unfortunately, I wasn't living here then. I had recently moved to our sleepy village of Bay Isles a year earlier. I used the small inheritance my granddad had left me and opened a café called Addicted to the Bean.

Today was the annual Spring Festival, complete with face-painting, fishing, egg hunting, and a giant bunny. Me. When I wasn't dressed as a funny bunny, I was whipping up lattes and pastries at my café.

"Why did I agree to this?" I muttered through the mask, complete with four-inch ears.

"If I recall, Todd talked you into playing the bunny for a few hours," Aurora said.

"Remind me to make Todd's lattes extra hot next time he comes in the café." I forced myself to maintain my stoic look, but my bunny mask hid my face.

"The kids are going to love you."

"We have kids in Bay Isles?" Based on my knowledge of my café customers, at least half the residents had an AARP card.

"Grandkids, great-grandkids, and a few young Millennials like us, but with kids," Aurora said. "Let's add more of these homemade chocolate eggs." Aurora emptied a plate of the candy into the large wicker basket. "And remember Mayor Clawson has given us extended opening hours at our first anniversary event. And he also promised a guest appearance."

"Mayor Clawson and his wife would have attended as our guests anyway, but the tradeoff seems appropriate."

"The community service is something our café could use." Aurora placed a few free coffee coupons in the basket and smiled. She wore a cute flowered top with jeans and white tennis shoes.

"Are these bunny-approved basket stuffers?" I tried to pick up a coupon. My concern about giving out the discounts was that my business had been slow.

"Yes ma'am, they are."

"I don't think children drink free cups of coffee," I said.

"They're for the parents. Believe me, Mo, every mother with a child under the age of ten will be grabbing handfuls of the coffee coupons. Now let's get you wiggling that awesome tail."

"That's easy for you to say, my friend. You're not the one wearing a fur suit. I just hope no one recognizes me."

"Well, speaking of that, isn't that Penny Jackson coming our way?" Aurora said.

I grunted.

"I gotta go help Granny Dee."

"Aurora, don't you dare leave me—"

Aurora had turned and waved her hand over her head before I had finished my sentence.

Of course, Penny, my wannabe-friend — well, when hell froze over — spotted me immediately. I groaned out loud. *Not Penny.* She and her clique of friends grew up in Bay Isles and reminded me of the Queen Bees and Wannabes from the film *Mean Girls.*

Penny Jackson click-clacked her Manolo Blahnik heels across the sidewalk. "Is that you, Molly Brewster, under all that fur? A little birdie told me you were dressing up today." She giggled.

"Yes. How are you, Penny?" One good thing about my mask was she couldn't see me gritting my teeth.

I glanced over my shoulder, but Aurora had briskly walked away.

"Well, I'm much better now that I've seen you dressed as a bunny." Penny covered her mouth to suppress another giggle. "How's the café business going? Every time I come in, you're bent over a mug of cappuccino. How do you move that milk pitcher to etch a design in the foam?"

"Takes a lot of practice." I tried to sound happy despite the sarcasm in Penny's voice.

Penny's superior, condescending mask momentarily fell. "Hey, do you have time next week for me to come by and talk to you about a business idea?" A flicker of distress flashed through Penny's eyes. Something I wasn't used to coming from confident and sassy Penny. *What business idea?* If I recalled, Penny helped her husband Jeff in his accounting business.

"Of course." I nodded my head with the slight range of motion I had with the heavy mask. My curiosity piqued.

Penny caught the eye of another one of her friends, Lucy, talking to a group of ladies.

"Has Lucy seen you yet?" Penny asked.

Oh no. The one person worse than Penny Jackson was her horribly stuck-up best friend, Lucy Lavender. "Uh…" I sputtered.

Before I could answer, Penny waved her hand and yelled. "Lucy, come here. Look who's wearing the bunny costume this year."

I could hear Lucy's chirping voice saying goodbye to the ladies.

"So, how does this Tuesday morning at ten sound?" Penny said. "At your café?"

"Perfect." I still wondered what Penny had in mind.

"And let's keep this between us," Penny said.

I nodded.

As if my furry rabbit costume wasn't enough of an embarrassment, Lucy wore a low-cut emerald green sundress that fit her figure like a glove. Her store-bought cleavage, thrust up and chasm deep, was displayed like grapefruit in the produce section. Every time I looked at Lucy, I thought about mermaids. I should mention that Lucy was once a Weeki Wachee mermaid, where she did live tantalizing performances in a tank, so she had that going for her. And wearing a green dress didn't help eliminate that image of her.

I knew Lucy couldn't wait to take advantage of my current costume state. I cursed Aurora and Todd, and even Granny Dee. Yeah, my Granny had encouraged my role at the spring event because it could be *good for business.*

My café business used to be booming. After I helped the local authorities solve a murder case a few months ago, my café was often visited by tourists wanting to gawk at the place where the fisherman was poisoned and to buy a cup of coffee from the sleuth owner who helped solve the murder. Lately, business had slowed down.

I took a sip of my water through a metal straw poked between the breathing slit in the mask, wishing it was something stronger. I wasn't feeling nearly as charitable as Aurora had implied, but I had to give it a big bunny try.

CHAPTER TWO

"Well, well," Lucy said. She cast a disgusted look at me. "Look who's wearing the costume this year."

For some reason unknown to me, these two women loved to pick on other women and poke fun at them. They enjoyed making me the target of their teasing comments from time to time. And my being a newcomer to the area played as the crucible of their crummy behavior — whether it was my red, frizzy hair or my less than perfect manicure, these two always found a weakness and exploited it relentlessly. Today, it was my outfit.

I planted my furry feet wide, but as hard as I tried, I couldn't keep my voice from sounding like it was coming out of a mouse. "Hello Lucy. Do you want a chocolate egg?"

Lucy rolled her eyes. While her friend Penny was the town's drama queen, Lucy was the town's evil queen of mean.

"No, thank you, Mo," Lucy said, sticking her slightly red nose up a bit. She had pale skin, the color of a fishbone, and perfectly coiffed bottle-blonde hair.

"Okay. How about your little ones?" I asked.

Lucy's two daughters trailed behind her. They appeared to

be close in age and dressed the same. I couldn't recall their names. They both wore identical baby-pink seersucker jumpers with embroidered yellow ducks over white pressed blouses. They were darling and impeccable. I'd give Lucy credit for that.

I pictured my own kids someday. And I had an image of a blonde boy with blue eyes, just like Drew's, wearing a pair of jean overalls with a bright-red checkered shirt. Of course, he would also be barefooted or wearing only socks, and one would be falling off and trailing behind him like a boat rudder.

"Sarah and Emily," Lucy said, "take a chocolate egg from the bunny."

The littlest of her daughters hesitated, but I smiled and nodded, realizing too late she couldn't see my smile.

Their little hands reached into my basket and retrieved two cellophane-wrapped chocolate eggs and placed them in their neon-pink plastic containers.

"What do you say?" Lucy insisted.

"Thank you," the oldest said, and when she smiled, dimples appeared on her rosy cheeks.

I mustered up a sweet, "You're welcome."

The littlest one bowed her head, afraid to look at me, the big bunny.

"Tank you," she said to her sneakers.

"Go find your cousins," Lucy said, shooing them away.

The children took off in a pack, running toward a cluster of other kids.

"I'll be there in a minute!" she shouted after them.

While Lucy watched them safely reach her sister Janet, I turned and prepared for a confrontation. You never knew what Lucy Lavender had on her mind. And with Penny hanging around, trouble was definitely in the wind.

Penny and Lucy flanked me, and I didn't know which way to turn my ginormous head.

Snickers, my loyal chocolate lab, made his way to my side.

When Lucy came close to me, Snickers wagged his tail.

"It's okay, Snicks," I said.

"Get lost," Lucy mumbled, adding a few other choice words under her breath.

"His name is Snickers, and he wouldn't hurt a soul," I said to Lucy/Cruella DeVil.

Ignoring Snickers, Lucy asked, "Where's your police officer friend? Has he seen you dressed like this?"

I winced. Lucy was referring to Deputy Drew "Lucky" Powell. Drew was a deputy at the Palma County Sheriff's Office in Bridgeport, a few towns over. His precinct covered the citizens of Bay Isles as well. Recently we had been on a few dates, and everyone in town called him my boyfriend. I'm not sure yet what I called it, other than we were dating.

"He'll be here later. He wouldn't miss this event," I said, feeling extremely uncomfortable.

"I'm surprised he can find any time at all with the boat thieves on the loose," Penny said, tilting her nose up smugly.

Boat thieves? I wasn't aware of a case that Deputy Lucky was working. "Uh-huh," I commented, glad they couldn't see my face flush.

Between Penny and Lucy, they knew everyone and everything going on in Bay Isles. And as an owner of the only coffee shop in the village, I heard plenty of gossip from the wealthy snowbirds and the tourists as well. But these two ladies in front of me grew up here and had their finger on the pulse of all the townies.

"Well, hopefully you'll have time to get out of that ridiculous costume before he comes." Lucy pointed her finger at the white ruffled apron wrapped around my furry waist.

"You shouldn't throw stones, Lucy. I seem to remember seeing a few photos on the Internet of you wearing a sixty-pound prosthetic fishtail, a green sequin bikini top, and tons of waterproof makeup," I said.

"I worked those mermaid shows before I met Clay. Besides, I liked being a mermaid. It paid well, and as a park employee, I was eligible for government savings plans. And all the swimming kept me in shape." To emphasize her point, Lucy smoothed her hands over her tight dress. "I'm sure your deputy boyfriend would rather see you as a mermaid than a bunny. But we'll see when he gets here."

I searched the lawn in hopes of finding some wayward kids to hop over to, instead of staying here and listening to their merciless teasing. And where was Aurora when I needed her?

On the other side of the lawn, Granny Dee was energetically maneuvering a group of children away from the picnic tables covered with potluck dishes. No doubt, fifteen types of potato salad, deviled eggs, casseroles, and Rice Krispies treats flowed from the plates being strategically positioned on the tables.

My grandmother, Edith McFadden, or Granny Dee, as most people called her, had perfected potluck organizational skills to a tee. She was waving her hands at a cluster of senior ladies, who nodded and began moving Pyrex bowls and Tupperware containers around.

I smiled at the thought of Granny. I'd gladly take her grouchy attitude right now over these two women.

I could hear Granny laugh, a deep, raucous laugh, reminding me how my grandmother could easily fill a house with lots of love and grumpiness. But as I looked toward where Granny stood by the picnic tables, I saw Aurora and Todd's sister Amelia with their heads together talking. Todd was nowhere around. Hmmm. I knew Amelia was a lawyer in Tallahassee and came to town to visit her parents often.

Aurora gave Amelia a bank envelope almost an inch thick.

Why would she be paying her? I knew it was none of my business. That didn't mean I'd stop wondering about it, though.

Amelia was a thorn in my side. Whenever she visited Bay Isles, she was always giving me a hard time. And I had no idea why. Todd, her older brother, was dating Aurora, and I had Drew. Maybe she was jealous because she was still single at thirty-three years old. But she was a successful lawyer.

I tried to focus on the two in front of me. "What do you know about the boat thieves?"

Penny shrugged. "I heard it from Jane. Her husband works at the High-and-Dry Marina. She told me that a boat was stolen out of a slip at the dock moored at the marina."

I looked at her inexpressive eyes. "Here in Bay Isles?"

We rarely had crime. Our community was located on a barrier island connected to the mainland by a drawbridge. The Palma County Sheriff's Department serviced Bay Isles villagers. The entire force, including the Chief, worked burglaries and assaults, as well as arrested drunk drivers, drug dealers, people who abused their spouses, and robbers. They mostly broke up fights, helped kids cross the street safely, and located lost pets. Last year, we had our first murder in Bay Isles, but that was rare.

"Yup, at the marina," Penny chimed in.

The High-and-Dry facility at the Bay Isles Marina housed boats in covered storage on racks inside a four-story warehouse.

"Uh-huh," I said, thinking about Drew and losing interest in talking to these two.

"We have a fast boat. It's a Sea Ray," Lucy cooed.

"Can you drive it?" Penny chimed in.

"What?" Lucy responded.

Yup. I had definitely lost interest.

"The fast boat. You know, the Sea Ray," Penny said.

"No, but Clay can run it fast."

I'd been around boats all my life, and I wanted to tell Lucy
— and Penny, for that matter — the Sea Ray they owned was a
cruiser, and it didn't go *fast*, and then I thought, *You can't teach
a cougar to sing.*

I noticed kids were beginning to gather for the start of the
hunt. A nice distraction.

"Look, they're starting the egg hunt." I pointed toward the
group of kids running and screaming around the park.

That did the trick. I watched the Wicked Witch of the West
and Cruella DeVil wander toward the group.

"You should reapply sunscreen. Your nose is turning red," I
yelled after Lucy.

Lucy placed her middle finger on top of her nose and threw
me a backward glance and yelled back, "You should be aware of
mosquitos because they're attracted to fur."

I sucked in a massive breath.

Lucy and Penny strolled away like they were runway
models on a catwalk. I thought to myself, *Am I evil to hope
Lucy's daughters come back with chocolate-covered hands and
wrap their arms around their mom's waist?*

Lucy stopped to talk to a man with salt and pepper hair.
While they chatted, he looked over his shoulder at me, then
back at Lucy, and nodded. He gestured my way and patted Lucy
on the shoulder, then turned in my direction.

The man looked straight out of an FBI most-wanted poster,
his harsh glare juxtaposed against the lawn filled with the children's bright and cheery faces. Something about the guy made
the hairs on my neck go up.

Why had everyone left me alone?

When the man approached, I calculated his age as mid- or
possibly late fifties and he wore scuffed, wing-tipped, lace-up
shoes. The shoes made me think of my dad, who would have
turned fifty this year. He would make sure his shoes were highly

polished before he went to a meeting at the Big House, as he affectionately referred to the FBI headquarters in Washington, DC.

This stranger's wrinkled dark pants, a white shirt, and those fraying shoes seemed out of place compared to the expensive, fancy watch on his wrist. Dark sunglasses covered his eyes, and he didn't utter a word when he came up to me. He was a scrawny fellow with a nervous Adam's apple. He smelt of stale cigarettes.

I began searching my deep apron pockets for bug spray or mace, just in case I needed to spray a bug.

The man cleared his throat and gave me a low whistle.

I gripped my basket tighter, using the pressure to hide my flash of fear. *Idiot.*

He moved closer to me. "Hm. Hm."

Now what? My heart pounded in my chest.

"Nice tail," he said.

Before I could reply, he tugged on my tail. *Was he trying to pinch me?*

I swirled around and knocked him to the ground with my wicked right hook and smacked him over the head with my basket full of eggs. My right hook was passed on to me from my Aunt Tammera, who had learned it from her next-door neighbor who'd had a career as a boxer. The instinct to dump the basket of eggs on his head was passed on to me from my Irish-tempered mother.

"Are you crazy?" the man yelled from the ground, rubbing his jaw. Chocolate eggs littered his hair and pant cuffs.

"I'm an Easter bunny," I yelled at him. "Not an easy bunny."

The man, having calmed down a bit, sat up. "Honey, you're going to pay for this," he said, inspecting a hole in his pant leg.

It was so darn hard to see through my mask that I didn't

notice the squished chocolate egg that I slipped on. I let out a squawk as I catapulted to the ground right on top of the man.

There we were, both tumbled on the grassy lawn.

"Get off me!" he yelled.

Out of nowhere, a Palma County Sheriff car appeared and drove up slowly, investigating the situation.

Just great! Deputy Drew's timing was impeccable.

"Everything okay here?" a deputy I didn't recognize said, as he tentatively walked around his vehicle. He had strawberry-blond hair that barely moved in the light breeze. Where was Drew? And who was this deputy?

"No!" the man answered.

"Yes!" I said at the same time.

The officer raised his eyebrows at the man on the lawn amid the scattered Easter eggs. Then he bent over and offered his hand to me.

"The bunny punched me." The man rubbed his jaw.

"Take off the mask," the deputy demanded.

I reached up and removed the bunny head.

"I'm Molly Brewster. Where's Deputy Lucky?" I asked, looking around and gasping in the fresh salty air. "And I only reacted to his hands pinching my ass —" I shook my head and sighed, "—my tail."

I tried to smooth my frizzy static hair flying in my face.

"Okay, Molly. Nice to meet you. We'll get this straightened out. I'm Deputy Drake Cross. I'm the department's new officer. I took Ted Walker's position after he retired." He extended his hand but realized my mitten paws prevented me from shaking.

"I think she broke my jaw," the man said, standing up and covering his mouth with his hand. "You'll pay for this. I want to file an assault charge."

"Calm down, sir. What's your name?" Deputy Cross asked.

"Jerry Ryder." He and Deputy Cross shook hands. "I do

freelance work for the island magazine. I was here looking for a human interest story. And I didn't pinch her." His eyes glared at me.

What? I shook my head. "Sure, you're as innocent as a choirboy," I said, trying to save a little of my dignity before it was long gone.

A small crowd of children and parents were gathering around.

"Why you little bitch—"

Deputy Cross interrupted Jerry. "Sir, no reason to call names. Let's get this sorted out without all the little eyes peering at us. Come on."

Deputy Cross turned and opened the back door to his patrol car. "Get inside. We can figure this out at the station."

Mr. Ryder and I escaped inside, with Snickers between us and an army of wide-eyed children staring at us.

There I was, in a grass-stained furry outfit, with frizzy hair and a mask-kissed face. All I wanted to do was spend the day at the beach reading Agatha Christie. Now I was sitting in the back seat of a police car with chocolate-covered hands.

As we pulled away from the curb, I heard a little boy say, "Look Dad, the Easter Bunny is getting arrested."

CHAPTER THREE

By the time I returned to the café, Aurora and Bales were both waiting for me by the front door where the taxi dropped me off, while the cowardly assaulter was probably back at Fort De Soto Park pinching another miserable somebody.

"Oh sweetie," Aurora whispered in my ear as she hugged me. "I bet you're starving. How about a muffin and coffee?"

"Sure," I said. "I'm exhausted."

"You'll feel better with some coffee in you," Bales said.

Coffee, yes, my head screamed.

Bales made the coffee while Aurora pulled freshly baked blueberry muffins from the oven.

"You know I could have come and picked you up." Aurora handed me a small plate with the muffin, while Bales set down a cup of fresh brew of the day with cream and a smidgeon of cinnamon.

"Thank you." I had calculated the greater evil: Aurora leaving the café during the lunch rush to pick me up versus a thirty-dollar taxi ride. When I had exited the police station, a few taxi drivers were on the front steps chatting. A bird in hand had won out.

"I needed you here at the café." It was true; either Aurora or I was always working. With me out for the later part of the morning, I needed Aurora to run the café while I was being questioned at the station.

"Oh, I was out anyway. Um, I had errands to run," Aurora said.

Her comment made me wonder who was tending to the café while we were both gone for hours.

"Let me toss the bunny suit in my office." Thank goodness I had the foresight to keep my work clothes in my backpack. I had changed into my unofficial work uniform of faded jeans and a brown t-shirt at the police station. It was bad enough driving in a police car dressed as a bunny. I didn't need the Black and White beach taxi driver staring at me on the ride back.

When I returned to the kitchen, I sipped my coffee, and I felt my headache ease and began thinking clearly.

My café's smells helped me relax with the freshly baked pastries and perked coffee. It was an aroma I loved from the moment I opened the front doors on our first day of business nearly a year earlier.

A basket full of jellybeans and Cadbury eggs sat on the white quartz countertop next to the old fashioned brass register.

I smiled at Aurora over the top of my coffee cup.

Since she became my partner, we had made a few changes to the interior. I loved how Aurora was always on the same page as I was, especially about the big things. We had different views about the café décor. I had fallen in love with the seaside look of blue hues and nautical accents, but Aurora would have had all Victorian antiques.

"What's more painful than being arrested?" Aurora blurted out.

I wondered what they knew about the incident at the park.

"Having to have your police officer boyfriend bail you out," Bales laughed.

"Okay. Funny. Technically, I wasn't arrested. We just needed a quiet place to talk," I said. "And Drew didn't bail me out. I left on my own."

I pulled an apron over my head and tied it around my waist. Sitting in the taxi, I had time to think about the events of the morning. I was usually a strong person and normally would not have worried about the incident with Jerry Ryder, but he had rattled me more than I'd like to believe. It was bad enough that he tried to accost me, but then to be accused of punching him for no consequence… He was an idiot, and I wondered if Lucy or Penny had put him up to it.

"Not until Deputy Lucky came galloping in giving his recommendation and offering to be a character witness," Aurora said with a mischievous smile on her face.

"I didn't see Drew." Officer Lucky Powell and our dating relationship had been a constant target for teasing over the last few months.

This place, Addicted to the Bean, was my lifeline and dream job. I felt so at home in my café. Tins of muffins baked in the ovens, espresso and latte machines chirped and burbled, and the aroma of scones filled the air. It was early afternoon on a Saturday, and the Bean was slow. We were serving a simplified brunch menu, which fulfilled the hungry customers throughout the day. Our excellent coffee and pastries weren't the only things that kept people coming in, but it was mostly the way we catered to the customers that kept us busy.

My café was ideally located in the picturesque seaside village of Bay Isles, where shops and local businesses were surrounded by the beach, bay, and boardwalks. It was walking distance to the beach and within 100 boardwalk steps to my apartment. Technically, my apartment was connected upstairs to the café.

"So Drew never got to see you in the rabbit costume?" Bales murmured, with hopes of igniting the teasing conversation.

"Thank goodness. What a relief," I said as I watched Aurora pull another batch of my favorite muffins from the oven. It was late in the day to be baking fresh pastries, but I knew Aurora had made them for me. I smiled at her. Her culinary skills rivaled Henrietta, Granny Dee's cook.

I could never manage to bake the blueberry muffins like Aurora. My blueberry muffins were always polka-dotted with purple patches and soggy berry blobs on the bottom.

Aurora nodded back at me. "I can only imagine that he'd find you adorable. What guy doesn't want to have a bed bunny?"

"Wearing that suit must have been fun," Bales commented.

"Easy for you to say. You're not the one still picking green lint out of your belly button," I muttered as I stepped from behind the counter.

I felt a renewed sense of energy, and I had only been gone half of the day. Deputy Drake had questioned us, and in the end, neither one of us wanted to press charges. I had offered him free coffee at the café. I had this same policy for all the men in uniform. We never took coffee money from the local deputies, paramedics, or firefighters.

How did I become the energetic owner of a café that also housed a book nook? I moved to the Gulf Coast town of Bay Isles after I inherited money from my grandfather, Lowes McFadden, my mom's dad. The great thing about my business is I get to be around my passion every day. I love books, and I love coffee. The bad thing about my business is I'm not a people person. I'm usually grumpy and can't even speak to people until I've had at least one and a half cups of coffee and a blueberry muffin. Then I can smile. But I don't do chit-chat until I've had my second cup of joe.

The café was coming up on our first anniversary. We had seen a lot of changes in the last year.

The most significant change was that my best friend in Bay Isles, Aurora, had become a partner in the café. Aurora was my first hire when I opened the café almost a year earlier. She worked part-time for me, mostly baking, and had a wedding cake business on the side while juggling online college classes.

She lived with her parents in a beachfront house on the island. Her dad was a dentist and her mom was a yoga teacher at the dance studio three doors down from the Bean.

It was nice to have Aurora and her family so close to my shop. Her dad was an excellent handyman, and I often called him to help with the café.

Besides Aurora, I only had my grandmother, my employees, a dog named Snickers, and a recently adopted Siamese cat, Kona, here in Bay Isles.

A month ago, Aurora and I joined forces. Aurora often worked the early morning graveyard shift at the shop. Her hours were off-kilter to the rest of the community. She worked from 3 a.m., when she mixed the first batch of scone dough, until noon. I often helped her open the shop, but after I locked the doors around 8 p.m., I was so exhausted I just wanted a hot bath and cold sheets. That routine killed all possibilities of dating.

My schedule had been a big reason I offered Aurora the partnership. That and her incredible baking and organizational skills. Well, and not to mention, my romantic life needed a boost. With Aurora around to help with the day-to-day managerial chores, I was freed up to date my favorite police officer, Deputy Drew "Lucky" Powell.

Drew often did twelve-hour shifts and occasional overtime at the station. For the last few months, our dates had dwindled down. As a deputy of our county, Drew chose to live in a town a good deal larger than the one I lived in. Besides having our crazy work schedules to maneuver around, we had a short commute to each other's places.

Although neither town was exactly a hotbed of murderers, robbers, and rapists, it appeared that Drew handled his share of jaywalkers, drunks, and family disputes.

I felt grateful he hadn't witnessed Jerry and me duking it out verbally at the sheriff's office that morning.

Aurora rolled her eyes and let out an exaggerated sigh. "Did I hear you gave the news reporter a busted lip?"

"Is that true?" Bales asked.

"He deserved it," I said.

"If you say so, boss," Aurora replied.

"Nice." Bales crossed her arms and winked at me.

"I'm afraid that the new deputy is going to think you have a bit of a temper, especially when you followed up your 'hey buddy, keep your hand to yourself' with your right cross," Aurora said.

I wondered why Aurora would even care what the new deputy thought.

"And don't worry about Drew missing out on seeing her in costume. I snapped pictures of Mo to share with Drew later. For now, let's tackle that pan of muffins in the oven."

Aurora loved gossiping, and she was happiest when she was chatting with the customers. She wore a smile every day and was a comic. I noticed the rhinestone comb she had worn earlier at the park was no longer behind her ear.

Bales slid a plate of muffins across the stainless counter and took a seat on the low chair next to Aurora. She chewed a wad of green gum, snapped it, and looked over a pair of reading cheaters the color of watermelon. Bales once told me she had 20/20 vision and wore different designer glasses every day to make her appear smarter and more sophisticated. She was 36 years old, divorced, and had a seven-year-old son.

I sank my teeth into the warm muffin. Aurora's baking was what dreams were made of, especially after spending hours at the police station talking to Deputy Cross.

The doorbells jangled, and I looked up with a ready smile. I saw Granny Dee, and when I noticed the woman behind Granny, my smile froze.

A tall woman with a straight back and a mane of long blonde hair talked to Granny.

I felt a cold expression cross my face as I stepped outside the counter. "Hi Granny."

And I looked behind her, and I met my old friend's eyes. "Hello Kathy."

"Hello Molly," replied Kathy coolly.

Kathy Waves and I used to be best friends. She was dressed in a long Pepto-Bismol pink flowing skirt with a tank top splattered with rhinestones. And despite the warm day, she wore brown studded cowboy boots. If Barbie came in a Mae West version, she would look like Kathy.

Great, I thought. *First, I had to endure Lucy and Penny, and then a bunny-pinching maniac, and now Kathy Waves wanders into my café.*

Lucky me.

A flash of hatefulness stabbed at me. But this was my café and given a choice, I would always take the high road.

"Come here and give an old friend a hug," I said, trying not to sound too apparent and shocked.

As I moved in front of Kathy, her expensive Chanel perfume stung my nose.

Kathy hesitantly hugged me. She pulled back and looked me up and down.

"I see you're still wearing man-repellant attire," Kathy laughed.

A sense of inadequacy swept over me. We were standing in my quaint, cozy café that held all my dreams. This place was my rock, my true source of strength this past year. And my baristas and the little family I had were supportive. This woman wouldn't just walk back into my life and ruin it for me again.

Aurora glanced at Bales, but neither of them said anything. Instead, Aurora pushed herself between Granny and me. "Hi, who's this?"

"Kathy and Mo were college roommates and good buds in middle school," Granny said.

"Well, nice to meet you, Kathy." Aurora extended her hand, and the two shook. "And Mo doesn't need to dress up like Dolly Parton. She has a great man."

Oh no. Aurora was moving into a protective mode.

Kathy bit her lip and tilted her blonde head. "Oh, she does?"

"Her guy is the real deal," Aurora continued, ignoring my shut-the-front-door stares.

"He's a cop. He's successful. He's strong, handsome, and sinfully sexy. He's so hot," Aurora said, beaming.

"Okay, enough. Kathy doesn't want to hear about Drew," I said.

"No, that's great to hear," Kathy said, looking a little uneasy at first.

"Did I mention sexy?" Aurora added.

"Aurora, why don't you make Kathy an iced coffee?" I asked.

"That would be great. And no sugar or cream," Kathy said. "The smell is murder in here. How do you not just sit here all day long and eat pastries and drink coffee? Well, taking another look at you, that's probably how you've added those extra pounds you're wearing."

Kathy, despite her delicate look and fake smile, could be a mean woman through-and-through.

"What brings you to town?" I asked, ignoring her comment. Her presence in my café gave me heart palpitations.

Kathy looked at me suspiciously, then said, "I'm here on family business. I just finished a meeting, um, at the park." I noticed a look of discomfort cross her face, and then Kathy added, "And Tom's in a surfing event this weekend in Bay Isles."

"Tommy — um — Tom's here?" I reached for my braid to tug then realized I had my hair in a ponytail, so I twisted that instead.

Kathy snorted. "Not here. He's at the hotel."

Granny looked at me. "And I thought those blonde extensions were real."

Kathy paused, seriously considering the comment.

"While you girls catch up, I'm going to make me a tea." Granny walked away.

Kathy squirmed around a bit. We were standing close to the antique sidebar, and Aurora, while preparing the coffee, moved closer to listen to our conversation. I glanced out the front door, and Snickers was lying on the front porch under the Dog Parking sign.

"How are you?" I asked.

"Good," she replied.

"And Tommy?" It hurt to know they were here in my town and she was in my café.

She mechanically ran her hand across her face and grinned. "We're great."

I couldn't hold back any longer. "I thought he dumped you," I said. "For what, the third time, was it?" I quirked an eyebrow at her, and I tried to keep my distaste for her from coloring my voice.

Kathy grimaced. "Only two times and hopefully the last." She flashed her left hand in front of me. "It's gorgeous, don't you think?"

Was that an engagement ring? My heart began to pound. There was a time when my entire life had revolved around Tommy Pierson. Those days were long gone, and with that breakup, I had lost my best friend. It had been a double whammy to my gut when I had caught Tommy and Kathy together.

Suddenly the café smelt briny, and my knees felt weak.

When I didn't comment, she flashed the ring in my face. The next moment moved in slow motion as Kathy was finishing her statement. I didn't hear her first sentence.

"I mean, well, whatever. It's not like it's a complete secret that we planned to be together one day, permanently."

When I didn't reply, Kathy kept rambling. "Well, I guess it all worked out." The glare she gave me intensified.

I swallowed hard and aimed to push Kathy's buttons. "Well, with me out of the picture, I guess it worked for you. And then there were Delaney and Courtney too, right? With them out of the way, he's all yours."

"What are you insinuating?" Kathy glared at me.

Before either of us knew what was happening, adrenaline got the better of the situation. Aurora bounced over, and when passing the iced coffee to Kathy, she held it up. I stepped to the side just in time, as Aurora dumped the cold liquid all over the front of Kathy's highlighter pink studded top.

The next few seconds were a blur.

CHAPTER FOUR

K athy yelled as the coffee splattered her top, skirt, and
boots. "You bitch!"

I could see Aurora's hand shaking. She backed away and
tried to set the cup on the sideboard.

"Don't you walk away from me," Kathy shouted. "Bring me
a towel."

"It was an accident," I said.

"The hell it was." Kathy bellowed. "That bi—"

"Is there a problem here?" Granny said as she swung around
from behind the counter.

"You're damn straight there's a problem," Kathy seethed.

"Calm down," I said, trying to place my hand on Kathy's
arm.

She yanked it away, unexpectedly smacking my jaw as
she did.

Instead of stepping away, I clumsily fell into her. We did a
dance, each taking a step, this way, then that. Before I knew
what was happening, Snickers was at my side, growling and
barking.

It all happened so fast. Snickers jumped up on Kathy. And

when she turned to flee, Aurora tackled Kathy and knocked her to the floor. The half-empty coffee cup slipped from Aurora's hands and spilled across the floor. I slipped. Aurora tried to help Kathy up. I felt a hundred pounds of bone and flesh and pink fabric pressed on top of me. Kathy smelled of coffee. So much for her Chanel.

All three of us were tangled on the café hardwood floor when the doorbells jingled. We all turned.

I could almost see Deputy Drew's mind spinning as he scrutinized the situation. He looked at the three of us on the floor, then he turned and slowly panned the room, shaking his head.

"Well, should I yell *freeze*?" Deputy Drew finally said. Drew studied me, and his look made me wonder if he wanted to arrest me or protect me.

Kathy's lower lip quivered, and she behaved more like I remembered her, with her big brown eyes filling with tears. That is to say, Kathy was increasingly melodramatic. "She started it, officer!" she yelled, pointing at Aurora.

"She's lying," Aurora said.

"Ladies, slowly disengage and stand up," Deputy Drew said, and extended his hand to me.

His lanky frame looked even taller from the floor. He was six foot two and built like a marathon runner, and his stealth-uniformed appearance commanded authority in any place of business. Right now, his curious grin and sparkling blue eyes bore down on me.

Kathy was plainly irked that he had offered me a hand and not her.

I perked up, even though it was the second time in one day that a deputy had to help me off the ground while covered with a gooey, sweet substance.

"Who called the cops anyway?" Kathy said, eyeing Drew in

his Palma County Sheriff's uniform and mirrored Costa sunglasses.

Embarrassed about everything that happened, but relieved that Snickers, Drew, and Aurora had come to my rescue, I realized at that moment that I'd never been more grateful for Drew to step into the café the instant he did. It could have gone so out-of-control.

I moved into him, and he stiffened. "Thank you," I whispered.

Kathy watched our exchange. "Well, if it isn't Mr. Sexy Cop," she spat out.

I turned toward my old friend and politely said, "Kathy, it's time for you to leave."

Kathy stood up and tried to smooth her skirt. She looked at her watch. "I have to go back to the park anyway, for a meeting."

She turned and glowered at Aurora. Kathy's face turned redder and redder, and when she looked at me, I thought her head might explode.

"God, I hate you. I always have. And I'm so glad I stole your man," Kathy said, her voice dripping with malevolence.

"Enjoy Bay Isles," I said to her back as Kathy walked out the door.

We all watched her as she stopped by the Dog Parking post and bent down and picked up the water bowl. Kathy poured the clear liquid on the wood deck. She flung the porcelain bowl at the pole, causing it to shatter, and then she stormed out into the parking lot.

Bitch, I thought. *A real bitch.*

Drew turned to me. "Do you want me to arrest her?"

I shook my head as I watched her drive away. "That woman has always been a thorn in my side but arresting her won't help.

Her fiancé is a lawyer." My heart sank when I thought of Tommy as Kathy's fiancé.

We were all quiet for several seconds, recovering from the Kathy incident.

"You okay, Mo?" Drew's voice softened.

I sniffled but nodded briskly. "I'm fine. Thanks, Drew."

"That woman is a menace to society, and I think you should file a complaint with this officer," Granny Dee said as she walked by holding a broom and dustpan. She winked at Drew.

"I think Aurora handled her quite well. Thank you very much," I said to Aurora.

There was a moment of silence, and then everyone in the café burst into applause.

"Good riddance," Aurora said, beaming.

Twenty minutes later, the café was back together. Granny had cleaned up the mess we had just made.

Deputy Drew had taken forever to finish the Bean's famous smoked ham sandwich on caraway rye with spicy Dijon mustard. When he did, he stood up and grabbed my arm and led me to my office before he said anything. When the door was shut firmly behind us, he sat on my desk and looked at me.

"Okay, Mo, what's going on?" The sad look in his gorgeous blue eyes wasn't helpful.

I took a deep breath and sat at my desk, acutely aware of Drew watching me.

"What?" I said.

"First, I hear you punch a reporter this morning at the spring festival, and now I find you wrestling with a tourist."

I smacked my hand on the desktop for effect, but it did the opposite.

Drew crossed his arms. "Well? What's going on, Mo?"

"First off, I punched Jerry as a reaction to his pinching my ass—tail. He pinched, I turned and slugged him. And second, Kathy is not a tourist. She's—" I stopped. What was Kathy? My ex-best friend who stole my boyfriend. Drew would never understand.

"She's what?" Drew asked.

I looked at him.

"Well?" he said.

I spilled my guts about my past with Kathy and Tommy. "We used to be friends in college. Good friends. And well, I was dating this guy, Tom, for a few semesters, and he and Kathy became friends, and I found out when I came back from a ski trip early. And, well, you know how the story goes. Now they're engaged, and she came to rub it in my face."

Drew merely stared at me as if I were babbling, and I guess he was right because I didn't recall what I had just said. It just came pouring out.

Why could this good-looking cop always get me talking?

I got up from my chair and began pacing, which was a feat in my tiny office. "Kathy was trying to get under my skin, and I guess things got out of control."

Sometimes Drew carried this strong, silent cop thing way too far. I stopped and stared at him. "Well, are you going to say anything?" Fine tufts of my ginger hair had sprung from my ponytail and hung down on my forehead like wispy bangs.

I brushed the hair from my eyes and turned away from Drew.

"You've had a busy day. I don't know how bad luck follows you, Ms. Molly," he said gently, touching my chin and turning my face to make me look at him.

That was when I started to cry. "I don't kn…kn…know," I whimpered. I was shivering from the air conditioning vent overhead pointed down on me.

Drew wrapped me in his arms. "It's okay."

I nodded and cleared my throat. Even though his embrace was warm and comforting, I stepped back. "I know you have every reason to be upset with me now. I mean, you being a deputy and all." I took a deep breath. "You see, I've known Kathy for a long time, and she hasn't always been this way. She was just…blinded by love. She used to be okay, you know. Even at a young age, when I lost my dad, she was always there. I owed her a lot."

"Yeah, but look what she did to you," Drew scoffed.

"I know," I said. "I guess she saw that I was that crazy, love-struck girl. She became jealous. While growing up, we'd been through so much together. When I was a teen, after my dad disappeared, my mom often went away to Italy, and I usually stayed with Kathy and her parents. She was always the caring, affectionate one. She loved to braid my hair, and she'd make cookies and lemonade. Kathy followed me to college. And she changed a lot when Tommy came into my life. I guess maybe that's the reason she's mean now."

I took a deep breath and went on.

"When I caught them together drinking beer at our favorite campus pub, they looked like a happily married couple, staring into each other's eyes." I shuddered. "It's like everything changed for us then."

"Did Tommy know about you two?" Drew asked.

I nodded.

"That creep."

"He always thought Kathy was a strong, independent woman. But he knew we had grown up together. It still stings." My voice cracked. "And now they're getting married."

Drew wrapped his arms around me again. "They deserve each other. Those two have no morals."

I slumped into his body.

Drew smashed me into his chest, his hand on the back of my head. It felt so good to stand there next to him. Feeling sheltered and protected.

I buried my face in his chest, trying not to cry. I exhaled and breathed in his musky smell. We stood awkwardly and cuddled for a few minutes, and Drew rocked me back and forth. Times like this made me feel so protected, and I wondered what life would be like as his wife.

"Everything's okay. That's over with," he murmured into my hair.

I should have left the moment alone, but I couldn't keep my pie-hole shut. "What's with these boat thieves?"

Drew grasped my shoulders and pushed me back, searching my eyes.

I shouldn't have asked. Ever since last year, when I helped solve a murder case in Bay Isles, Drew had been very sensitive about his investigations.

He tipped my chin up, so I looked into his bright blue eyes. He seemed so sincere and determined I couldn't breathe for a moment. "You sure you're okay?"

I nodded and gave him my best grin.

"Mo, I think I've found a good lead to something." He led me to the chair. "Sit."

He pulled a small notebook from his pocket. He leaned over me, our legs touching, and pointed to the numbers on the page.

"Does this mean anything to you?"

"They look like email addresses." I stared at several letters, then an underscore, with a few numbers followed by the "at" sign, but not a dot com.

His hand touched mine and held it. "Not just any emails."

"Are they from Mexico?" I noticed the missing domain address ended with just a .mx.

"Bingo."

"What do Spanish email addresses have to do with anything?" Was Drew sharing information with me regarding the boat thieves? And if so, why? In the past, he made it clear he didn't want me snooping around his investigation.

He flipped another page over. And I saw a series of numbers.

"Are those numbers longitudes and latitudes?" I asked, excited, and hopeful that he was sharing his case. This had to be related to the missing boats.

He smiled.

"I don't understand." I stared at the numbers again.

"You know, by using coordinates of degrees of latitude and longitude, we can name any point on the Earth's surface."

I nodded and bit the inside of my lip. Then I got it! "Isn't that Bay Isles Marina?" I recalled the coordinates from my boating lessons last fall. "The High-and-Dry?"

"Yup."

"So is this related to the boat thieves? And what are the thieves looking for?" But as I asked Drew, it occurred to me. "Maybe something is hidden in a boat? And they're not stealing the boats to pawn off for quick cash. The thieves are looking for something."

Drew's eyes widened. "That's what I think."

I blew out a breath. "What the heck is hidden in these boats?" I had to find out what boats were being stolen to determine if there was a pattern.

"Think about it. Spanish emails."

"Drugs? Drug money? Or a long-lost Spanish treasure map?"

"Those are as good as guesses as any," Drew said, shutting his notebook.

"But who sent the emails? And where'd you get them?"

"We have forensic working on that. For now, the big question is, what were they looking for in the boats? And if there's a pattern, we need to be guarding the marina. I have a security guard watching it day and night. And Brad is installing a camera security system this weekend. This whole boat thief thing has a lot of questions without answers."

"It's a mess, I agree." Nothing like this has ever happened here in Bay Isles. Why this town? Why this marina? Why not steal boats from a more extensive marina, I asked myself? Then it occurred to me that all of these boats from the High-and-Dry marina were not a coincidence.

"Part of the reason I came here, besides to see you and have lunch with my favorite barista," he smiled and continued, "I'm here to talk to you about your granddad's boat."

"The Sea Ray Sundance? What about it? I haven't taken his boat out for a while. I've had Brad at the marina come over to Granny's a few times to flush out the engine, but I haven't been on it in a few months."

"It's the same type of boat the thieves are targeting."

"And you're worried that whatever they're looking for, it's valuable enough to look at all Sea Rays? Including ours?"

"I'm just concerned. The Sea Ray is at Granny's house?"

I nodded. "It's in the boat garage."

"I'd feel better if you secured it at the marina versus her house. I've brought in McNulty from Bridgeport to watch the marina in the evenings."

"Amos McNulty? Isn't he retired by now? He comes in here from time to time after fishing."

"He's old enough to retire, I suppose, but he still handles a few shifts here and there. More security details."

"You know he'll sleep through most of the graveyard shift."

"Fine with me. The presence of a police officer and his car is what we need as a deterrent."

Amos McNulty reminded me of an old dog my neighbor

had. He was a hundred years old and had three teeth left but still managed to gnaw the meat off bones. The neighbor's dog, not Amos.

"I'm glad your men are on it, but I'd like to take a look at the boat first, then I can move it to the marina." I wasn't sure what I'd be looking for, but I had to take a look.

"I can help you."

"I'd appreciate any assistance you can offer," I said, trying not to act excited. With Drew's relationship with ICE, he had learned a lot from the Immigration and Customs Enforcement team, and he could thoroughly search any boat.

"Can I meet you at Granny's tomorrow?"

"I look forward to it."

Drew's cell phone rang.

"Deputy Powell," he said into the mobile.

"Uh-huh." His eyes widened in surprise. "Got it. On my way."

He hung up and looked at me.

"What? Another boat's missing?" I asked.

"Penny Jackson's German Shepherd, Gucci, was chasing a bunny into a wooded area at Fort De Soto Park and—"

"— and what?"

"She found a body."

CHAPTER FIVE

"A body?" I asked. My heart began to race while my mind tried to picture the festival this morning. When I had left, most of the kids and parents were winding down. What had happened?

"Whose body did she find? Anyone we know?"

"Yes. Evidently you know him."

"Him?" My heart pounded faster.

"Jerry Ryder."

"The reporter?"

Oh no. My concern was more at the thought of someone I just met having a heart attack than for the man himself. "A heart attack? Stroke? Or maybe drowned?"

"Slow down with the questions, Mo. And get your backpack. You're coming with me."

"Me?" I was surprised he'd want me to go with him. "Why?"

Usually, when Drew was on official police business, he didn't want me anywhere near the case. In the past, my sleuthing activities made him nervous. And following him and sneaking around to find clues seemed to cramp his style.

That's why I was pretty shocked to hear Drew wanted me to tag along.

"Why am I going?" I repeated.

"Penny refuses to talk to the detectives until she sees you."

"Me?"

"She was pretty adamant. Putting you, as usual, in the middle of my second murder case."

"So he was murdered?"

"I'm not saying anything more." Drew held up his hands.

"Did Penny say why she wanted to see me?"

"Nope."

"Did she say anything?"

"She's pretty hysterical."

"Do you think she knows something about Jerry's death?"

"Inappropriate question for me to answer."

"But you want me to talk to her?"

"Maybe you can calm her down. And get her to talk to us. No one there can calm her. And since you two seem to have a certain flare between you, I thought you could help calm her down."

That was all the explanation I needed. I grabbed my backpack. When we came out of my office and made our way through the kitchen, I saw Aurora talking to Bales behind the counter. It was late afternoon, and the Bean was empty, except for my two baristas and one elderly couple.

I started to think about what Drew was proposing. I had a knack for digging into people's lives. When I looked around the café, it was quiet. A murderer on the loose would be bad for business. If the killer wasn't found quickly, the Bean and other businesses could be hurt by the loss of tourists. As it was, the cafe was operating on a shoestring.

I walked up behind Bales, as I heard her say, "I'm just

dotting the I's and crossing the T's, that's all. If Penny found the body, then I'm just questioning her involvement."

"Well, if you're going to get pissy about it, then maybe you can dot and cross somewhere else, that's all I'm saying," Aurora replied.

Had they already heard the news?

When they saw Drew and me, they both stopped talking.

"Are you on your way to Fort De Soto?" Bales asked.

"But how—?" I knew gossip traveled fast in our little town, but unless they were eavesdropping on our conversation, I couldn't believe they'd already heard.

"We heard it on the police scanner. Someone was found dead in the park," Aurora said.

It had slipped my mind that I kept a police radio in the kitchen. "I'm going with Drew," I said.

They nodded and didn't act one bit surprised.

"Where's Granny?" I looked around the café.

"She left as soon as she heard the news. She mumbled something about having to help clean up the potluck tables."

"And you let her go?" But I knew once Granny got something in her head, there was no stopping her.

"Yes," Aurora said.

I shook my head.

"Let's get going," Drew said.

We walked past the elderly couple, Jim and Marge. We said our hellos. As we walked out, I heard Marge say, "Jim, really, another cupcake?"

And Jim replied, "You know I can always use the afternoon pick-me-up, with my fluctuating blood sugar."

"Give me a minute," I said to Drew. I stepped behind the counter and quickly made a large iced chai tea latte with a sprinkle of raspberry.

Drew rolled his eyes when he spotted the drink.

"Can I bring Snickers?" I asked as we stepped out onto the porch. "He's good with scents and intuitions."

Drew looked at Snickers and nodded.

"Okay. Let's go."

Snickers wagged his tail as I hooked the leash on his collar. "Let's go for a ride."

On the six-minute drive to the park, with the flashing red lights on, but no sirens, I asked Drew more about the body.

"Was it an accident?"

"No."

"What happened?" I was fiddling with the air conditioning vent and Drew looked over at me often. Maybe he was concerned that I might flip on the siren instead. The thought had crossed my mind.

"A knife in his neck," Drew said, glancing over at me.

"What?" The announcement didn't exactly land like a bombshell Drew intended, but I was surprised. Definitely interested in who might have stabbed him.

"Evidently, it was a sharp little thing. It caused a lot of blood loss, but thankfully it wasn't serious."

"So he didn't die?" I was relieved. Even though Jerry Ryder was a miserable, bunny-pinching man, he didn't deserve to be stabbed to death.

"No, he's dead all right." Drew stopped at the small bridge to let a family of ducks cross the road.

Snickers stuck his head out the window and growled at the fowl as they waddled past.

"You said he didn't bleed to death. Then how did he die?"

"Looks like he fell after he was stabbed and hit his head on something. That's what paramedics think killed him. The bump to the head."

I gasped. After the initial letdown of the stab not killing him, I hadn't seen that coming.

"He fell on a rock, or he was clobbered over the head with one?" I asked, thinking to myself how earlier I had wanted to clobber Jerry on the head with more than chocolate eggs.

Drew glanced over at me. "Too early to tell."

As Drew drove past the giant flagpole where only six hours earlier Jerry had been alive and pinching, I thought about who would want to stab or bludgeon him to death.

"Well, as sad as that is," I said, "I don't understand how someone could stab a man in board daylight, and no one see it happen. This should be an easy case to solve."

Drew shifted uncomfortably in the driver's seat. I could see his face go red.

"I agree," he finally said, as we drove down the vintage red brick roads that ran through the center of the island. The thousands of resident gopher tortoises often used these streets.

It always felt neat to think that horse-drawn carriages used to shuttle soldiers and their families to the beaches on these same red brick roads.

I worried now if the reenactment event would be postponed or cancel. Every spring, the park, in cooperation with local Bay Isles and other counties, hosted a Battle of Ballast Point Civil War reenactment. The participants depicted both Union and Confederate infantry, artillery, and civilians. This event would take place next Saturday.

Today had been the egg hunt and picnic for the children and their parents; next weekend was the reenactment for the history buffs.

The reenactment also included period sutlers and vendors, a mock military trial and execution, artillery demonstrations, infantry drills, a lady's tea, and drum and fife music performances.

But a murder investigation, once again, in Bay Isles, could trump the event.

As we pulled close to the fort buildings, I noticed two State Police vehicles near the path entrance. They must have just arrived. I pointed them out to Drew.

Drew hopped out of the car and quickly strolled over to the officers. I stayed back and found myself and Snickers standing alone on a tiny island of calm while pandemonium went on around me.

Then I spotted Penny.

She looked like a tiny mama bird surrounded by her brood. Her dog, Gucci, lay at her feet. She held the hand of her youngest daughter, who looked bored. Another daughter twirled her dress and tried to do a cartwheel.

Despite my dislike for Penny, tears welled in my eyes as I watched her herd her dog and daughters to a picnic table.

When she spotted Drew approaching, her face began to quiver. He walked over and put his arm around her and let her lean into him.

Out of the corner of my eye, I saw several officers talking to EMTs as they collected supplies from their ambulance. One paramedic I recognized, Kevin, sprinted toward the brush and disappeared into the wooded area behind the yellow tape.

The cloudless denim blue sky seemed incongruent with a dead body hiding in the brush.

Deputy Cross moved his cruiser to the park entrance, where he parked to form a barricade and was telling the gawkers to calm down and stay put.

I waved at him, but he returned a frown. *Great.*

I watched Drew steer Penny in front of a State Police car. When he took out his notepad, Penny burst into tears. Drew exhaled and nodded over at me.

"Let's go, Snickers," I said as we walked across the grassy lawn toward Penny and Drew.

Gucci perked up and smelled Snickers, and then the two

ignored each other. I noticed Gucci was off her leash and wore only a collar.

When Penny spotted me, she collapsed against Drew again in fresh weeping.

Based on Penny's lackluster greeting, I wondered if Drew had been wise to drag me into this. Maybe her favorite latte would make her feel normal again, if only for a short while. I knew all too well how it felt to find a body and then to have an army of officers wanting to take a statement.

I pulled a fresh travel packet of Kleenex from my backpack and handed it to Penny. She didn't thank me, but she nodded, pulled one out, and blew her nose loudly into the tissue. I couldn't help thinking all this drama and attention suited her well.

As if reading my mind, Penny grinned slightly with her red, watery face.

I handed the large iced chai tea latte with raspberry to her. "Just the way you like it. I thought you could use a little caffeine therapy right about now."

She grinned and nodded. "Yes. Thank you."

I gave Drew a look, and he stepped back.

"When she calms down, I need to question her," he whispered to me.

"Okay," I whispered back and nodded my head sideways towards his cruiser.

I watched for a few seconds as Drew walked over to his vehicle.

"Penny, Drew said you wanted to see me. Why?"

"You have to know how I feel."

"Yes, I do know how it feels. When I found a body on the beach last year, it was horrible." It had been a terrible sight finding a body washed up on the beach. What was happening to our sleepy little seaside village? Two bodies in twelve months.

She nodded and sniffled, then sipped the latte. Her face softened as the creamy caffeinated drink hit her.

"What happened?" I hedged, hoping she'd open up to another pedestrian-finding-a body. But I was still the bunny she made fun of this morning too.

"You didn't see anyone do this, did you?" I asked.

Penny opened her mouth and then snapped it closed, shaking her head. "I should never have gotten that knife from the pie platter." She sniffled and blew into another Kleenex.

Had she brought the knife? "What knife?"

"The knife I used to slice the strawberry pie. Mary Dedham made it. It's the same recipe that won the Palma County baking contest. It was amazing."

"Okay." I glanced over at Deputy Drew, who was leaning in his cruiser, talking on the radio.

From where I stood, he looked mighty fine.

"And where was Jerry?"

She looked at me like, *who's Jerry?*

"Um, the body," I said.

"Oh no. I didn't see him. I had used a kitchen knife earlier to cut Gucci's leash." She shuddered. "I wish now I hadn't."

I tried to move Penny's story along before Deputy Drew or another officer came over.

"You saw a body in the bushes when you cut her leash?"

"No. I mean yes. I cut the leash. I saw Gucci chase a bunny into the brush, and that's how she got tangled. She dragged her leash in there." Penny pointed toward the brushy area that was now roped off with the yellow crime scene tape.

"So you didn't see Jerry—um, the body—then?" It was better not to call the victim by his name.

"No. I saw nothing. I went back to the kids. But ten minutes later, Gucci ran back toward the bushes again."

I placed a hand on her arm. She looked horrified, then glanced at the deputies and relaxed.

"I don't have to go to the station, do I? I have to finish cleaning the park, go home and bathe the kids, and then make dinner."

"Don't worry about that now. There're plenty of helpers that can clean up. And I can have Henrietta make dinner and bring it over. She makes a ton of food every night anyway." It was true; Granny's cook and housekeeper Henrietta cooked enough food to feed a small army.

Penny nodded.

"So when you chased after Gucci the second time, where was the knife? And how long had it been?"

She looked at me, sniffled, and twisted her lips. "I said it had only been another ten minutes or so."

"Is that when you found…it?"

She nodded. "At first, all I could see was something red. The grass was matted. Gucci was growling at it. I thought maybe it was a dead bunny."

She stopped to brush fresh tears from her cheeks. "It wasn't a dead bunny." Penny bit her knuckles, quivering at the memory.

"What was it?" I knew what it was based on what Drew had told me a few minutes earlier, but I needed to hear from her what she saw.

"It was his hair! The back of his head. I didn't stay around to find out if there was a whole body connected to the head. I ran out screaming."

She shuddered and held the Kleenex to her mouth like she was going to toss the award-winning strawberry pie.

She stopped as she suddenly remembered something. "Hey, you went to jail with the reporter this morning. Did you come back here and stab him?" she asked breathlessly.

I studied her for a moment but remained silent. I was rarely at a loss for words. But I'd better listen to her if I wanted to learn what happened. I shook my head slowly.

"Really? Who the hell would think I had anything to do with the dead guy?" I said incredulously. "Don't be ridiculous. I didn't kill anybody. You've always been imaginative." I didn't want to end up in the interrogation room of the Palma County police station again.

I paused, gazing at Penny while collecting my thoughts. "I have to ask this—did you have anything to do with Jerry's death?" I asked bluntly.

"No!" she responded adamantly. "How can you even ask?" Penny smoothed her already perfect hair, bobbed precisely to her chin.

"You asked me the same thing two minutes ago."

"I know you didn't do it. Just like you know I didn't," Penny said, throwing her head back.

"I don't know that. From what you're telling me, the police are going to find your fingerprints on the murder weapon."

"I told you I cut Gucci's leash with it."

"I find that plausible, but I can say that the police may not."

She chewed on the tip of her thumbnail.

"And you found the body," I added, knowing all too well that discovering the body could make her a suspect.

"My dog found it chasing a bunny. That doesn't mean anything."

I had no reason not to believe her, aside from all the evidence the police would have on her.

I sucked in a big breath. "Tell me everything. Start from the beginning. Did you touch the body?"

"No."

I could read people well. I had a lot of aunts around me, growing up. My mom and her five sisters lived all within a mile of us in Oregon. My Aunt Tamera had taught me how to tell if someone was lying. "Are you sure?"

Penny sighed. "I checked his wrist for a pulse. And there wasn't one."

"What about the body temperature when you touched him?"

"Still warm."

"No sign of anyone — anything?"

"I screamed. And then I yelled for help. Dr. Dodgson came running over."

Dr. Rick Dodgson was the local vet, and therefore a lot of people in the community respected him for his medical training. He once saved a cherished resident's Oscar fish from the final flush. Dr. D, as the locals called him, performed surgery and removed a tumor from the fish's head. Living in Bay Isles, he had successfully accomplished quite a few specific pelican, fish, and sea turtle surgeries.

"Other than Dr. D, did you see anyone else?"

"Everyone came running over, but the new deputy and the vet kept them all back."

"Anyone seem out of the ordinary?"

She hesitated and glanced her eyes downward, and the next word out of her mouth was a lie.

"Nope."

"Are you sure? What did the crowd do? How many people were here?" I knew she saw something. I looked at her two daughters sitting with their next-door neighbor. "You would want your girls to always tell the truth."

She looked at her daughters. "Well, there was one thing."

I handed Penny her drink that she had placed on the picnic table. She took a sip.

"Tell me everything."

"Okay. When Deputy Cross came running over. He calmed the gathering crowd and said, 'I regret to inform you that there appears to have been'" – Penny cleared her throat – "'an accident.'

There were a lot of murmurs from the crowd. And he told everyone to stay around because the State Police would be here soon and might want to interview them. Everyone started talking at once. I turned around to walk back to my girls, and I noticed a tall female leaving the crowd."

"What did she look like?"

"Long blonde hair. I couldn't see her face, but I remember she just seemed odd."

"Odd how?"

"She had on boots. And it's so warm here. The temperature has to be in the eighties today. Who would wear boots to a park?"

"Boots? Like what type?"

"A cowboy type with studs on them."

"Was she wearing jeans?"

"No. She had on a pink dress."

I knew someone who wore boots and a pink skirt. Kathy.

———

After ten minutes, I walked over to Drew, who stood at the open door of his cruiser, one foot on the running board, microphone at his mouth.

"She's all yours." I gestured toward Penny.

"They've found another boat missing," he said when the voice at the other end paused. "All hands were on deck here at the park, and another boat has turned up missing from the marina."

"How long ago?" I asked.

He held up a hand and listened to the fuzzy transmission. "It's hard to tell. Maybe an hour."

My thoughts went back to the murder. Could this be related? There were only a few ways on and off our island. There was the Ten-cent bridge that connected Bay Isles to the mainland, and then there was an exit by a water vessel. Could the killer have stolen a boat to avoid the bridge? Cameras monitored the bridge. And possibly the killer knew this.

"Do you think it's related to Jerry's death?"

"At this point, I don't know what to believe. Let me talk to Penny now. She's okay to speak to?" he said, a bit nervous.

I nodded.

"Can you get a ride back to the café?"

"Yes."

"I'll call you later. We need to compare notes on what Penny told you."

I nodded again and knew I had been dismissed.

Snickers and I went in search of a ride back to the café. And I had to wonder if my fight with the victim earlier in the day would put me on the suspect list.

CHAPTER SIX

My intent in visiting Granny Dee was to make sure she was okay with moving Grandpa's Sea Ray boat to the guarded High-and-Dry Marina, as Drew had suggested.

I had driven my golf cart over to Granny's seaside house.

Even though I loved my tiny one-bedroom loft apartment, I felt warm inside every time I came to Granny's house.

Growing up, I'd searched all fifteen rooms of her house, annoyed her cook Henrietta by being under her feet in the kitchen, and climbed and descended enough of the stairs in the house to give me cramps. But my favorite part of the estate was the backyard gardens.

I parked the golf cart in front of one of the garages and walked through Granny Dee's backyard. It smelt like freshly mowed grass and the sea, two of my favorite smells. The garden contained umpteen pots and urns brimming with flowering herbs, bushes, and ivies, and was possibly the most beautiful place on the island. This backyard was Disney World to a gardener.

Whenever I was dealing with the mint plants, I had to wear gloves and a mask. I was allergic to peppermint, especially fresh mint. This odd allergy had actually helped solve a murder in Bay Isles a few months ago.

I pushed the back door open and was immediately hit with the warmth radiating from the oven and the familiar smell of a mingled blast of ground meat and onions.

"Hello," I yelled out. "You really should keep this door locked," I said to the empty kitchen.

Snickers immediately searched the tiled floor for crumbs. The kitchen was located on the ground floor of the three-story residence and was fashioned after a country house, with a back staircase that accessed the upper floors.

It appeared as though Henrietta had started dinner preparations and then been called away mid-execution. The shiny chrome eight-burner stove still radiated heat, chopped parsley wilted on a cutting board, and pie dough ballooned out of its bowl. A cast-iron skillet simmered on low heat with a meat concoction, the source of the enticing aroma.

I pushed open the heavy swinging door that led from the kitchen to the dining room. When I entered the dining room, I stumbled over George, Granny's Siamese cat. George, named after George Clooney, replaced Elvis, her fourteen-year-old Siamese, a few years ago.

George looked up from washing his face, meowed once and went back to it.

Snickers sniffed George then continued his search for crumbs. George ignored Snickers. The two got along fine; however, George despised my mother's two pets, Roco and Bullet. Roco was mom's tan, feisty Chinese pug and Bullet was her silver cat with a green eye and a brown eye that scampered about faster than a speeding bullet. The two pets had visited a few months ago and all hell had broken out in Granny's house. It didn't help that my mom dressed her pets in holiday costumes.

I walked past the wall that boasted a gigantic gilded mirror and happened to catch a glimpse of my own face. The golf cart ride had caused my red hair to come out of its ponytail, and my bangs were sticking up at odd angles. I ran my fingers through my bangs, attempting to fluff and tame them.

I made my way to the connecting living room. Snickers trailed behind me nose to the floor as he walked.

After my granddad Lowe passed away, Granny had redecorated the house. The living room was now a muted shade of grass green with Scandinavian folk art paintings. Granny sat on an insanely comfortable purple plush couch covered with zebra-skin throw pillows. The room was striking, but it could make you a bit dizzy at first, like you'd just woken up with a hangover.

"Didn't you hear me yell?" I said as I spotted Granny perched on the sofa opposite Henrietta on the loveseat.

Granny stared out at the empty space between the purple sofa and the wall like it was her enemy. Her lips were pursed, and her pale gray eyes squinted.

"Granny, I need to talk to you about the boat," I said.

"Shhh," Henrietta said, pointing at the bookshelves, where the cherrywood cabinet doors were flung open, and an old computer with speakers squawked the latest police radio conversations.

I shook my head in dismay. "Does everyone listen to police scanners?"

Police radio scanning on the web had been one of my grandfather's hobbies. In our small town, usually a phone call to Christine, the police station dispatcher, would be enough to know what was going on. But Granddad Lowe would listen to live audio broadcasts of police, EMS, fire, and even the railroad and aircraft communications. He had an FCC license, and he had taught me how to download the station. I could listen to the Bay Isles, Bridgeport, and

Palma County Sheriff's Department police reports live. One could say I was spying on my love interest at work. But I not only had a knack for making killer lattes and pastries, I also had a knack for solving crimes. This was the reason I listened to the police scanner.

"When did you start listening?" I asked Granny.

"Hi Mo." Granny finally acknowledged me. "After last year's murder, you bet your sweet iced tea that we listen in occasionally."

I walked over and gave her a kiss on the cheek. Snickers rubbed his head under her resting hand until she petted him. Then he turned and went to Henrietta and lay down at her feet. He knew who dished out his meals.

"How are you, Ms. Mo? Have you had dinner? Are you hungry?" Henrietta asked, giving me an affectionate smile.

Henrietta Filadora was Granny Dee's cook. Not only was Henrietta her long-time live-in cook and housekeeper, but she had recently taken on the role of caregiver. Although she was not officially trained as a caregiver, she offered to take on the extra duties. After all, she was at Granny's side every delicious breakfast, lunch, and dinner. She was known for serving authentic Italian dishes with a modern touch. Last night she had cooked a creamy and flaky Italian pot pie.

"I'm starved," I replied. "Do you have any leftover pot pie?"

This pleased Henrietta, and a broad smile filled her face. She loved making the McFadden and Brewster households clean their plates.

"Nuts! You no eat leftover pie. It'll be too soggy. I feed it to Snickers. You stay for dinner, yes?" Henrietta's language resorted to her Italian heritage when the talk of food or murder was involved.

With the mention of his name, Snickers' head perked up. He didn't care how soggy the pot pie would be.

"Yes, I'd love to stay."

"I make a fine ham loaf and ham balls with the leftover pork roast, ham butt, and ground beef. I ground up meat in the grinder. We eat no leftover pot pie tonight."

Henrietta put ground beef in nearly everything, from her addictive appetizers to her famous family lasagna, to even her breakfast casseroles.

I smiled warmly at Henrietta and then glanced around. I noticed the half-empty glasses on the coffee table, a bowl of mint and lemons, and a sweating pitcher of iced tea with a few slivers of ice cubes.

"Did you send the casseroles over to Penny Jackson's house?" I asked.

"I had Jet drop them off," Henrietta replied.

Jet Mitterhammer was Granny's gardener.

I heard the radio crackle.

"It was that reporter," Granny said with a sigh.

I nodded.

"Oh Molly, dear." Granny turned to me with a concerned look. When she used that expression, her thin lips puckered, and her forehead crinkled with lines. "I'm so relieved you didn't find the body."

"Me too." I had found the body of a dead fisherman one morning while jogging. He had turned out to be poisoned, and I helped the police, without their approval, solve the murder.

"So maybe, Miss Crime Solver, you could do me a favor," Granny said.

"Not if it involves prying into Drew's police business," I said but thought it was too late for that after talking to a hysterical possible suspect for him.

She shook her head and made a tsking sound. "I know you'll get involved. That's just your nature. But tell me, why were you talking to Penny at the park after she found the body? And why weren't the police talking to her?"

I looked at her, narrowed my eyes, and then walked over to the computer and turned the speaker sound on low. How did she know I had talked to Penny? "How much does that scanner tell you?"

Granny removed her cell phone from her rose-colored shirt pocket. "Marge called and said Jeannie talked to Rita and Rita's granddaughter goes to school with Penny's oldest daughter and—"

I sighed and held my hand up. "Okay, all I can say is... Penny insisted she talk to me first and Drew asked for my help, that's all."

"Is the department going to hire you to help interview suspects?"

"No, they are not. Penny was hysterical and wanted me there. And who said she's a suspect?"

"She found the body, didn't she? Was it murder or natural causes? When I saw that reporter earlier this morning at the park, he looked like a walking heart attack waiting to happen." Granny picked up her tea glass and took a tiny sip.

"Well, it sure as heck didn't look natural to me," I said. "Unless you call a knife stabbed in his neck and a smash on the head natural."

Both ladies gasped.

They sat there speechless.

Granny finally said, "Another murder?"

I nodded.

"But who would do that?" Granny asked.

"The police are searching the crime scene now. Did you see anything unusual today?"

Granny twisted her mouth and had a funny look on her face that prompted me to ask again.

"What is it, Gran? Is something wrong?"

"No, it's nothing, dear."

"Anything from this morning that stood out?"

Granny rubbed her chin, and I could almost hear her thinking. "It's really nothing."

"I'm looking for anything. Did you see someone talking to Jerry, the deceased reporter?"

She looked up, frowning. "No, not him. It's just something I noticed."

"What?"

She waved her hand. "It's probably nothing."

"What?" I was losing my patience, and as much as I wanted to think I'd stay out of the investigation, I knew I couldn't. Besides, eventually, the police would interview everyone at the park that day to see if they saw anything out of the ordinary. I was just a few steps ahead of them.

"It's something that I noticed regarding Penny."

"What might that be? Was she talking to Jerry? Arguing with him?"

"No, you're the only one I saw argue with him."

"He pinched me. So yes, I punched him." Did everyone in Bay Isles know we argued?

"Come on, Dee," Henrietta chimed in. "Tell Ms. Mo what you saw."

"I'd seen Penny's toenail polish before," Granny said slowly.

"Her nail polish?" I still didn't see where this was going.

"Not her nail polish, but her toenails. The color. It seemed—" Granny hesitated.

"What did it seem? And what does it have to do with anything?"

"The color matched Kathy's."

"Kathy?" Just saying my ex-best friend's name gave me

pause. She was a horrible person, but we had been friends once. She seemed so different now. She had been bitter and jumpy at the café earlier today.

"Yes, I noticed Penny's nicely pedicured toes in her fabulous Manolo Blahnik sandals. I thought, *How does her husband Jeff make enough money as an accountant to afford the likes of the designer shoes she is wearing?* I know there's the designer shoe warehouse in the city, and there's the outlet mall over the Sunshine Skyway bridge but the—"

"Granny, the toenail polish?"

"Oh yes, dear. It was a perfect match to Kathy's."

"Why would you think that? And so what?"

"Don't you see? Penny's matched her plum-colored top, that exactly matched her lipstick, and the paint on her perfect oval fingernails and her slingback heels was the same shade and her —"

"— her toes matched the nails. But Kathy?"

"Her toenails were plum too, with that little glitter sparkle," Granny said with excitement in her voice.

"So what? Penny and Kathy go to the same nail salon."

"No, Kathy said she just got into town today."

"Maybe they have the same taste in nail polish." But I recalled the last time I'd seen a manicurist, I had to choose a color from a wall of about a thousand bottles of polish. It was overwhelming.

"But Kathy wore pink," Granny said. "Her outfit today was pink."

I was beginning to see her point. "Wait a minute. Kathy had on boots. How do you know her toenail polish color?"

"When I walked from the parking lot to the café, Kathy was sitting on a patio chair shaking out a boot. She said she had a rock in her boot. I saw her toenail color then. I thought to myself, *Who doesn't wear socks with boots?* And then I thought,

I've seen that polish color before. And how I'd like the color for my fall pantsuit. You know, the one with the ruffled, puffy sleeves? Wouldn't that color match nicely?"

Henrietta bobbed her head and nodded.

I thought about this for a minute, seeing a simple kind of logic in what Granny was thinking. It could be a coincidence, or it might be worth a visit to the local nail salon.

I rubbed my chin. "I wondered why Kathy wore boots in the warmer weather. And her fingernails were a gaudy hot pink. But her toenails matched Penny Jackson's toenails. This could be just a coincidence." But the thought of these two getting pedicures together irked me. Still, I saw no connection to Jerry Ryder's murder. Except for the fact that Penny described Kathy this morning as someone she didn't know.

"Well, you asked me if I spotted anything unusual."

I wasn't a girlie-girl, but even I knew a dark plum color was a bit unusual for the spring. "It wouldn't hurt for me to stop by the Island Salon and see if Dana carries that color." I had a day off tomorrow and had little else to do. I knew Drew would be tied up with boat thieves and now a murder to investigate.

"What made you think of these two women when I asked about Jerry's murder? You said you thought of Kathy when I mentioned suspicious. What else besides her toenail polish?"

Granny took a big swallow of her tea, wiped the condensation from her hands with a napkin, and said, "With the article Jerry wrote about her family last year, wouldn't that make Kathy hate him? Maybe not enough to kill him. But Kathy said she just got to town, and yet she has an odd connection to Penny with their —"

"With the colorful toenails," Henrietta said excitedly.

"What article?" I asked.

Granny looked at me. "The one about Kathy's family business. That reporter is a sleaze. Jerry Ryder takes advantage of people's bad luck and writes his so-called human interest stories that always end poorly. He wrote an article last year about Kathy's family. It had a huge negative impact on their company. I read somewhere later that her brother ended up divorced shortly after the business downfall, and her dad fell ill."

"I'll have to research the articles Jerry wrote. But if he focused on people's ill luck or their business demises, then he could have lots of enemies."

"I don't know about a lot of enemies, but I would focus on Kathy. And whoever else he was in town to see."

"I'll google his articles. But it would be helpful to know what he was working on. I saw him talk with both Penny and Lucy this morning. He told Deputy Cross he was at the park to do a human interest story on the festival."

"Hmm. That doesn't sound like the articles he writes."

"I'll have to find out where his office is and pay the editor a visit. If I can find out why he was in town and who he wanted to interview, that may be a start. I'll find out more about Kathy's family's business too. And when she got to town."

"Text Dana and ask her," Granny suggested.

The Island Salon, located a few doors down from my café, was owned by Dana Moneymaker. We were fellow business owners and friends.

I pulled out my cell phone and sent Dana a text. After I hit send, I poured a glass of tea. I still had to discuss the boat with Granny.

A few minutes later, Granny had agreed to let me take the boat to the guarded High-and-Dry, but not before Drew and I searched it.

My cell phone chimed, and I received a reply from Dana.

"Looks like Penny had a pedicure yesterday."

"Oh?" Granny said.

I typed a quick reply. *Was she with her out-of-town friend? Kathy?*

And waited.

Dana's reply came within seconds. *She was with a tall blonde. Not sure of her name.*

I typed, *I loved their nail color. It was plum-colored. What do you call it?*

Dana's text reply said, *Get Cherried Away.*

Granny scooted over on the couch and leaned over my shoulder and read the last text.

I looked at Granny. "You were right. Penny and Kathy know each other. And Kathy lied about when she arrived in Bay Isles."

Granny nodded. "Kathy has a motive. And it appears she's been in town long enough to have a matching-nail-polish-pedicure with Penny. Why would Kathy lie about just arriving in town today?" Granny said.

I shrugged. "Bottom line, Granny, we've got her nailed."

CHAPTER SEVEN

I t was close to eight o'clock when I pulled the golf cart in front of my apartment located behind the café. I had sent Aurora a text and asked her to feel free to stop by after she closed the Bean.

I would usually pull the cart into my small garage, but it was crammed with odd pieces of antique furniture, restaurant fixtures, and enough filled sandbags to block the Hoover Dam. Granny had insisted I keep the sandbags on hand. I hadn't been able to park a car, let alone a golf cart, in my garage since Hurricane Irma swept through.

I trudged up the one flight of stairs to my baby blue painted front door with Snickers trailing behind me. He stopped to eye a small pale green lizard clinging to the wall.

"Snickers, that's an anole. We didn't have these little guys where you were born."

Snickers and I still had a lot to learn about Florida. I had moved to Bay Isles just under a year ago. There was a lot of Floridian wildlife that was so different from Oregon. I didn't particularly care for the lizards. But Granny said they ate mosquitos and other small insects, and Lord knows Florida could use fewer mosquitos. I'd been in Granny's garden near the water at night and thought the mosquitoes would carry me away.

I kicked off my flip flops just inside my front door and headed for the kitchen, my feet as tired as the rest of me. I laid my backpack on the kitchen table.

Snickers went directly to his water bowl and lapped up a few mouthfuls. Henrietta's leftover pot pie must have been too salty for him.

My recently adopted long, slender Siamese cat, Kona, came out from under the curtain and rubbed along my leg.

"Good evening Kona," I said.

Snickers came running over and sniffed the cat. Kona raised his back.

I reached out my hand as I spoke to Kona and stroked his head. Kona purred.

"What happened to the shy, raggedy alley cat that I used to feed outside my café?"

Kona ignored Snickers' sniffing and purred and rolled over and meowed.

"You flirt. You think we've been gone for a week, versus eight hours."

Kona twisted his head to look at me, hopped up, then circled my leg and led me toward the kitchen.

"I bet you're hungry."

I followed Kona to my tiny kitchen. Like the rest of my home, it was decorated in soft island colors; hues of aqua, blueberry, and turquoise accented the kitchen towels and seaside accessories in my apartment.

I reached in the cupboard and pulled out a can of Fancy Feast. "Yum, savory turkey tonight."

Since I rescued Kona, he had gained four pounds. "You keep eating like this, and I'll have to call you fat cat."

I removed the food from the can and dumped it in a bowl.

Kona jammed his long nose into the bowl of turkey mixed with crunchies.

I rummaged in the refrigerator and found a cold beer. It had been a long day, and a cup of hot tea wouldn't calm my thoughts of Jerry dead in the bushes. Not to mention that I now knew that Penny was lying about not knowing Kathy. She had said a lady with long blonde hair and boots had been at the park but acted like she didn't know her. Yet Dawn confirmed that they had a pedicure together. Even Kathy had lied about coming into town today versus yesterday. What was going on?

Kona, delicate in his eating habits, paused between mouthfuls, gently brushing his whiskers in case some food was on them. As was our ritual, Snickers sat at my feet. We both watched Kona eat.

When I had found Kona a few months ago, he was a mangy mess. He was a stray that showed up behind the Addicted to the Bean café one early morning. I often fed him tuna and leftovers from the café. He would not eat until Snickers and I both were inside the back kitchen door. Then he ate and left.

Where he went during the day, I had no idea. I started calling him Kona because of his caramel coloring and the coffee grounds that clung to his whiskers and fur. Dr. D, the local vet, had said he was clearly supposed to be black with blue eyes, but instead, his coat was a reddish-brown color. The dark fur covered Kona's sides and back as well as his tail, face, and feet; everything else was a cream color.

I took my beer and plopped on my comfy leather couch. Kona jumped up, stretched, yawned, and lay down. Snickers chose a spot under my feet.

I turned on my laptop and summoned up the Google search bar. Jerry Ryder was a common enough name that the search yielded 586 results in 13 states. I switched over to images and shuffled through dozens of photos and then skimmed through Twitter, Facebook, and a few other social media sites, trying to match his face.

Instead of finding him that way, I added 'reporter' to the search bar next to his name.

"Bingo," I said. "Jerry Ryder isn't even his full name." I read aloud to my sleepy dog and cat.

"Jerry Ryder Mistack is an American investigative reporter for the Herald-Ledger, a newspaper in Tallahassee, Florida. He writes human interest stories, with an emphasis on the business and hidden stories.

"'Having Jerry show up in your town is worse than having Jim Cantore show up,' one local anchorman commented."

I had learned last year while waiting for Hurricane Irma to arrive that if the person on either side of you is The Weather Channel's Jim Cantore, prepare for a storm of biblical proportions. If Jerry Mistack was investigating in Bay Isles, there must be something big going down.

I read a few of the leading headlines;

Jerry Mistack, a former CNN network journalist writes controversy articles;

Jerry makes local man squirm in cringeworthy interview;

Jerry Destroys Local Business on Misplaced Bank funds, and on and on.

From the articles I read, Jerry Mistack was not a man you'd want in your area. I knew all about Southern hospitality, but Bay Isles Mayor Clawson should not welcome him. *A little late for that,* I thought.

I searched the records for the name Kathy Waves. Nothing came up associated with that last name and the dead reporter. I recalled that Kathy's parents had split when she started college. Would her brother take on another name? Or what if Granny had mistaken Kathy for another college friend?

I scratched my head. I looked at Kathy's Facebook page. We weren't friends on Facebook, but it gave me all of her aliases. Finding the right Kathy was like finding a needle in the Facebook haystack.

I had just popped the top off the second bottle of beer when I heard a hard knock at my front door.

Kona sprinted off the couch and to the window facing the bay and jumped on the sill. He didn't enjoy visitors and preferred to watch them from his safe perch on the windowsill. Snickers stood up and gave a diminutive bark.

"It's ok, Snicks. I bet it's your pal, Aurora."

"Hold on, Aurora," I yelled.

I glanced at my watch: 8:30. It must have been a slow night. She usually didn't stop over until after 9 pm. Most evenings the café closed at 8.

I swung open the door to see Deputy Drew standing there.

I stared at Deputy Drew "Lucky" Powell, looking tall and rugged in his once perfectly pressed uniform.

"Can I come in?"

"Of course. I was expecting Aurora, but this is a pleasant surprise." I opened the door wide. He stepped in and walked immediately to the couch. I noticed the lack of a hello kiss, which could only mean one thing; he was Deputy Lucky and not Drew, the guy I'm dating.

"Would you like a beer?"

"I'd love one, but I'm still in uniform."

"Cookies? I have some of Aurora's chocolate cookies."

"The ones with chocolate chunks and chocolate sauce dripped over them?"

"Chocolate ganache."

"Gahn ahsh?"

"The sweet, creamy chocolate mixture she uses for frosting."

"Yes, please. And a glass of milk."

I went into the kitchen and opened the refrigerator, hoping I had milk.

The carton felt light when I picked it up. I smelt the contents, and it passed. I poured the milk into a glass and piled four cookies on a plate.

Despite being delighted that Drew had stopped by, I had to wonder if he came to talk about the murder investigation. And if he did, what should I tell him?

I looked at the reflection in my refrigerator and ran a hand through my hair, then made my way back to the living room, happy to see Drew sitting on my sofa.

"We can eat in the kitchen if it suits you," Drew said.

"No, this is fine. You look relaxed."

"It's nice to rest. I've been going non-stop since Jerry's body was discovered."

Before I could answer him, he leaned over and placed his arm around my shoulder. Then he stifled a yawn.

"You sure you don't want a cup of coffee?"

"No, I've had plenty today. I'm on dinner break, and I have to be back at the office to research another call about the mur... der –" he stopped.

"You're not going to share anything, are you?" I wondered if I should tell him about the nail polish. And Kathy's lies about just getting into town. But I really didn't know if these two things had anything to do with the murder. So by not saying anything, I wasn't really withholding crucial information.

He looked down at the cookie in his hand, then raised an eyebrow at me before taking a big bite.

"Delicious, aren't they?" I grabbed a cookie, broke it in half, and popped it in my mouth. I took a swing of my beer.

"How do you do that?" He nodded toward the beer.

"What? Drink beer with cookies?" I held a cookie in one hand and a beer in the other. "This is a well-balanced snack," I quipped, balancing both with open arms.

He smiled and brushed a few crumbs from his mouth. "No, not that. How do you always seem to question my investigations?"

"Sort of a knack, I guess," I said, between rich, creamy chocolate bites. "I'm used to a faster-paced life, and in Bay Isles, I get bored. Plus, you asked me to talk to Penny."

"That I did. But not by choice. She demanded it. But you got her to talk more than she would at the station. You do have a way with people. You're a coffee shop owner, not a detective, but you have the skills to snoop."

I twisted my mouth back and forth. "Hmm. I'll take that as a compliment."

"And possibly a warning. Be careful, Mo. Please try and stay out of the murder investigation." Drew's voice was firm, yet compassionate, and I found that both sexy and worrisome.

"You don't really mean that, do you?"

"Yes, I care about you. And I don't think it's safe snooping around, not to mention it's a police matter."

"But a few months ago, after I helped solve your murder case, you told me I was good at it. And you also said I was a complex woman."

He smiled and looked directly at me. "That you are."

"And you said you liked that." I touched his arm.

He moved in and captured me in a warm hug. Even after his long day, I could still smell his aftershave, conjuring up an image that I found totally sensual. His big, powerful embrace was so comforting that I stayed a bit longer than necessary.

When he pulled back, he hesitated a few seconds, studying my face, his eyes now serious above his flushed cheeks. "At first, I wanted to run for the hills, or the ocean, in this case. But now, for once in my life, I want to learn more about you and figure out what goes on in that pretty red head of yours."

"Then it's settled."

"What's settled?"

"I'll agree to help you but stay out of your way."

"You know that's not what I meant." His eyebrows rose.

There was a loud crash as Kona jumped from the windowsill, landing on the coffee table and knocking over my beer bottle.

Kona, usually friendly with Drew, glared at him and hissed as if he'd understood the entire exchange.

Drew laughed and tried to pet Kona.

"I guess my adopted house cat agrees with me."

Drew blinked, shook his head and stood up. "I really should be going."

"But we work so well together," I said. "On so many levels." I wanted his approval of my helping.

"We do. But do I need to remind you—"

"—I'm a café owner, not a detective." I shrugged and stood up, feeling the usual tsunami of doubts about getting involved in the case come flooding in.

"Look Mo, you're amazing and intuitive. And from what I saw this morning, I liked the way you handled Penny. And then there's the murder you helped solve last Christmas." He paused. "You're really good at the investigative stuff. But please let me do my job."

I nodded but I mentally had my fingers crossed. I needed to help him, and for Penny's sake, I wanted to find out whatever it was that Penny might have gotten herself mixed up in.

Drew leaned in for a soft kiss. It was so delicious it made my toes curl.

Watching him go out the door made me feel a tinge of regret and sorrow.

If I ever lost him, it would be entirely my own damn fault.

CHAPTER EIGHT

When I walked into the Bean the next morning, a sense of frenzy filled my café. It was the week before Easter, and both the vacationing families and the college-aged kids with their money, appetites, and suntan lotion were flocking to Bay Isles and the nearby beaches. The tourists mixed with the locals made for standing room only.

A handful of college-aged guys in their colorful boardshorts, polo shirts with reptiles and mammals stitched on the chest, and topsiders flirted with Aurora and Bales, my baristas. I shook my head. It was before 10 am, and the guys were already out looking for a good time.

Aurora flashed me a glance, and I nodded to her. I was anxious to talk to her. She had sent me a text after Drew left last night and said she was too beat to stop by, but she wanted to discuss a plan she had the next morning.

Aurora with a plan could mean a lot of things, from bungee cording off a crane at the beach to sneaking backstage at a concert to hunting down a wild alligator, but mostly it involved hitting the thrift shops and putting together a crazy outfit or disguise to wear.

I had hustled into the café, vowing to get my paperwork done so I could go to the hotel and question Kathy before Drew stopped by Granny's house to search the Sea Ray boat. But my hopes of getting anything done were dashed by an unusually large crowd of customers at the café.

I stopped to talk to a family I recognized from the last winter break. They were from Ohio. After a polite exchange of pleasantries, during which they declined my offer to refill their coffees, they asked me, "Have you gotten any leads on who killed the reporter?"

A few eavesdropping customers cast their eyes on me.

I shook my head, feeling conspicuous. "Um, I, I'm leaving that up to the authorities."

"But with your relationship to the deputy and your involvement in the last crime here, we just thought you'd be able to tell us more about what happened," the mother said. She looked worried and concerned.

"I'm not a detective. But I'm sure the reporter knew the person who did this, and there's no reason to worry." I smiled and eyed the young children at the table.

"What else do you know about it?" a lady at the table across from the family asked.

"I know everyone in Bay Isle is shocked by what happened." I couldn't bring myself to say murder. "It's being thoroughly investigated by the police, and I have every confidence that the perpetrator of this terrible crime will be apprehended quickly." I sincerely meant that, so business could get back to normal.

"Come on, Mo," Mr. Shafer said. "That sounds like a press release. What's your boyfriend saying?"

"I haven't discussed this with the Sheriff's department." That much was true. Drew didn't tell me much of anything about the case last night. He did text me a few hours ago saying he had worked all night, and he'd stop by Granny's later this afternoon.

"What about the boat thief?" A fisherman asked.

The café was abuzz while customers peppered me with questions that revealed various levels of detailed knowledge of the crimes. It always amazed me how small-town gossip spread like wildfires in the Santa Ana foothills.

I neither denied nor confirmed anything. But it was hard to gloss over the murder. Especially when I found the last body and because I had been instrumental in solving the crime.

"I heard that reporter was a slimeball, and he did nothing but destroy lives with his written lies," Mr. Shafer commented to the group.

"There's probably plenty of people who won't shed a tear over this," another person said.

Aurora came walking over to me, a thin smile on her tanned face. She looked at the congregating customers and lifted her hands in surrender. "We're selling half-priced pastries for the next thirty minutes."

That caused a slight stir in the crowd, and I winked at her and nodded my approval.

Aurora was wearing her café uniform of black capris, a short-sleeved shirt, and a gingham apron and black wedge sandals. The apron was dusted with flour and coffee stains. Aurora stood two inches taller than me when she wore heels and I didn't. She usually wore her white tennis shoes.

She handed me a coffee. "Can I see you in the office?"

"Good morning," I said with a grateful smile, relieved to be summoned away.

"Excuse me," I said to the family of four as I turned away.

I followed Aurora, saying hello to groups of customers on my way back to the small office.

She shut the door and leaned heavily against it. "It's been like this all morning."

I collapsed in the chair. I could feel my face turn red, and I struggled to control my emotions.

"Are you all right?" Aurora asked.

I nodded but bit my bottom lip.

"Tell me the truth," she said, fixing me with a stern gaze.

"You know me too well." I rubbed the corner of my eye.

"Look Mo, you don't need to take the worries of the town on your shoulders."

"I know that. It's just that it's such a peaceful place, and it seems that bad things keep happening."

"But you can't control it. You had nothing to do with the stolen boats, right? I'm guessing."

I nodded.

"And you didn't stick a knife in Jerry's neck or hit him on the head, right?" Aurora asked.

"Of course not." I pushed my hair off my face, wondering how Aurora knew the cause of death of the murder victim.

How did I explain to Aurora what I was feeling?

"I want to make a difference in this town. I was good at helping solve the murder a few months ago, and with that came a feeling of strength and belonging. I can't really describe it. But it gave me a sense of being a part of this town, and Granny felt it too. She told me so," I said.

"It gave her purpose," Aurora said.

"Yes, that's a good way to put it. Granny told me yesterday she knows I won't be able to stay out of investigating the crime."

"I know you, and Granny's right, you won't be able to stay out of it. You can't let go of something that makes you want to help."

"But I'm torn between getting involved in the mystery and my relationship with Drew."

"You're afraid if you get involved, you could lose him?"

"Yes, something like that." I felt tears welling up in my eyes.

Aurora placed her arm around my shoulder. "He cares a lot about you. He knows you want to help. You will find a balance. We all care about you. And I will help you in any way I can. You know I will."

I sniffled. "Thank you for being such a good friend." I meant it. Since I'd moved to Bay Isles, I'd been so fortunate to have wonderful people in my life. Granny, Henrietta, Drew, Aurora — they all genuinely cared for me. I never had this feeling before. My dad and I had been close. When he was gone, my mom grew distant. Today she traveled a lot and came to visit Granny and me a few times a year. My mom meant well, but she lost the loving mother instinct when my dad disappeared and later was presumed dead. Aurora and Granny were the closest I had to family here.

"What's the plan then?" I said.

"The plan is to get you a disguise to wear." Aurora circled the desk, opened the office closet door, and pulled out several boxes.

"Disguise for what?"

"You can't go snooping around Kathy's hotel looking like you, now can you?"

I smiled. "I guess not."

"Try this one on." Aurora held up a red, black, and yellow diagonally striped minidress.

I slipped off my brown shirt and stood there in my black jogging bra and skinny jeans, eyeing the dress.

"Go ahead, slip it on," Aurora said.

I wiggled and squeezed the dress over my head and down my body. I pulled off my jeans. The dress ended mid-thigh.

"This leaves such a massive amount of my legs showing that I'll probably get arrested for being a prostitute."

"We can add fishnet stockings if you don't want skin showing."

"Great. If you have white leather knee-high boots, I can show up at Kathy's beach hotel dressed as a 60s go-go-dancer. That won't get attention."

Aurora buried her head in the box and pulled out a tan short-sleeve vest and a safari hat.

"What do you think of this?"

"What is that? Sherlock Holmes? Do you have a pipe, monocle, and magnifying glass too?"

"No. Not a detective, although that is sort of ironic, don't you think? But how about one of those Sea Turtle patrol people?"

She had a point. I'd seen them wearing their hiking boots and tan forest ranger-looking outfits early in the morning while out jogging.

"If we had a patch to put on the vest, that might work." I hated wearing dresses, but I could tolerate the brown shorts and a vest.

"I can make a patch. I'll pull a logo from the Internet of a nearby estuary, and we can draw it on paper and transfer or glue it to the vest. You can even wear your brown shirt underneath."

"I can hide my hair under the hat and wear glasses. And I could go to the hotel and mention that I had talked to someone that said they found a turtle nest. I'll describe Kathy."

"You can use this." Aurora held up a long blonde ponytail.

"Where's the rest of it? It looks like a mermaid was scalped."

"It doesn't matter. I can staple the blonde pony to the hat. Your red hair will be tucked up under the hat. So what do you think?" Aurora asked.

I examined the ponytail. "Although I am partial to my flame-red hair, I've always wondered what it would be like to be a blonde."

We were interrupted by a tapping noise on the office door that I recognized all too well... Granny's cane.

I threw the hat and blonde ponytail into the grocery bag and tossed it on the desk.

I opened the door to see Granny standing there, face flushed and looking very unlike herself – almost haggard. And shaken.

"Hi Granny, when did you get here?"

"That's not important. What is important, is, um, there's been an incident," Granny burst out with no sign of Granny's usual calm and grumpy tone. She was a full octave higher than normal. "We have a problem."

"What?" I replied.

Granny's voice rose another few notes. "That bitch is back." She sounded like a violin string about to snap. "And believe me, she is meaner than ever."

"Now what?" I scrambled up from the desk.

"She's a mess," Granny shrieked.

"Who?" Aurora and I both asked.

"Kathy. And it was *really* an accident," Granny said.

I felt a buzzing around my temples. "Oh no, what did you do?"

"It was her fault. Old man Wesley was trying to get his walker by Kathy, and she tripped on it. She claims she twisted her ankle, and she's threatened to sue you."

I looked at Aurora, and we both shook our heads.

If Granny was flipping out, I didn't want to make things worse by asking stupid questions. But I had to wonder, what would Kathy be doing here? This could save me a trip to the hotel. Maybe I could get her alone and ask her questions.

Aurora raced out of the office. I followed her, and Granny was behind me.

I immediately saw Kathy crumpled on the floor, bent over, examining her leg. For Pete's sake, why didn't Kathy watch where she was going? She was always ending up on the floor of my café.

However, a sprained ankle could be the entrance I needed to talk to her about the pedicure with Penny. What did Penny and Kathy have to hide? And what was their connection to the dead reporter?

Aurora reached Kathy first. I could see the smile quivering on Aurora's lips as she approached the sprawled-out Kathy. Aurora reached down and offered a hand to her.

"I'm so sorry about this. Granny said you slipped. Let me help you up and get you settled on a chair before the whole town sees that tiny strip of tickly pink lace creeping up your crack."

Kathy gave her a nasty look. She had on a tight-fitting swimsuit cover-up, but it was doing a poor job of covering up anything under it. She held one of her sandals, three-and-half inch heels with a one-inch platform wedge, in her hand.

"I think it's broken," Kathy whined.

I was more interested in her plum-colored toes. What had Dawn called it? Get Cherried Away?

Out of nowhere, first Snickers came over and licked the sweet coffee off Kathy's shoes, then Kona jumped out of the window box and popped into the café. He instinctively lapped at the spilled coffee with cream around Kathy's chair.

Kathy muttered a few choice words before a large tan arm reached out and squeezed her shoulder.

I took a deep breath as I came face-to-face with Tommy Pierson.

"Hi Tommy."

"Mo?" His face spoke a thousand kinds of confusion as he turned his eyes toward me.

"Yes, how are you?" I stared at my ex-boyfriend. A knowing smile carved deep dimples in a handsome and a bit browner than was fashionable face. A new scar slanted above his left brow. His ocean blue eyes, under blonde hair, bleached white from the sun, blinked a few times. He wore the familiar college-boy grin and outfit. He had on pressed khaki pants and an orange striped polo button-down starched so stiff it probably could stand up by itself without a hanger. The last time I saw Tommy was when he was walking across the Quad arm-in-arm with Kathy.

"What are you doing here? I mean, I heard you moved back to take care of Granny Dee, but I didn't think we'd run into you."

Kathy beamed and hurried to straighten up and planted a big kiss on Tommy's cheek.

"Hey baby, didn't you know Mo works at the coffee shop?" Kathy sniped.

"She owns it," Aurora said.

Tommy turned in the opposite direction of Kathy. He looked at me, then around the café. He nodded and said, "You own this place?"

"Yes, and these are my friends. This is Aurora."

"Hi Aurora, Tom Pierson." He extended his hand.

"Hi, nice to meet you," Aurora said, shaking Tommy's hand.

Snickers barked, and Kona circled my leg.

"And—" I reached down and picked up Kona. "This is Kona, and that's Snickers." I pointed to Snickers and held Kona to my cheek.

"You have a cat?" Tommy asked.

"Yeah, originally, he was a stray that I fed from time to time.

I tried to find the owner, and no one ever claimed him, and Granny—"

"Get that cat away from me," Kathy said as she pushed her hand in my direction.

Tommy turned to look at her in surprise.

Kathy quickly hid her outburst behind a big fake smile. "I guess you should know I'm not really a cat person, honey. In fact, even Maverick hates me."

"Maverick?" I stared at Tom's worried eyes.

"He's this little brown Ragdoll, and he's super catty. He can jump off a two-story house and land on his feet," Tom said.

"So you have a cat too?" I asked Tommy. The name of his cat hadn't escaped me. *Top Gun* was one of our go-to Netflix movies. I always told Tommy I'd get a hall pass for one night if Tom Cruise, who played Maverick, ever came to town.

"Yup. My German Shepherd doesn't seem to mind having a cat around. And Maverick doesn't eat much. But enough about me. How are you doing? You look great." He eyed my so-bland outfit.

Kathy stepped closer to Tommy, and I swear Kona hissed at her like a snake.

"Is that Tommy?" Granny Dee's voice crackled from behind us. She brushed her flour-covered hands on her apron as she scuttled over to the group.

"Mrs. McFadden. It's so great to see you again." Tommy hugged Granny so tight, I thought I heard her bones crack.

Granny smiled at Tommy warmly and stared at him. Her curly gray hair was neatly caught up into a bun, and her curious blue eyes peered over oval glasses sitting at the tip of her nose. Her expression read, *What the hell are you doing here with her?* as she glanced one eye over at Kathy.

"What are you doing in Bay Isles?" Granny asked.

"There's a surfing event," Tommy said. He absentmindedly

reached over and petted Kona, gently cradled in the crook of my arm. Kona purred, while Kathy simmered.

I placed my cat on the floor, and Kona scampered out of the café. With the front door open, the spring air with low humidity held the fragrant smell of the flowering vines climbing the stucco walls of the café. A seagull made a landing on the patio table looking for crumbs, and Kona made a beeline toward it.

Snickers, also tired of the human talk, left to park himself outside on the café porch.

When the animals were gone, the adults turned their attention back to the conversation.

"I didn't know you surfed," Granny said.

"Me either," I added.

"I do surf, but I'm not here to do that. I'm here with a friend who's a professional surfer. I'm here to represent him on some legal paperwork for a movie he's filming. I haven't been in the water in months."

"Where would your friend surf? I didn't think Florida had waves big enough. Besides, it was smooth as glass yesterday," I said.

"You're right. We're here to do promotions," Tommy said.

Kathy looked at her manicure and, looking bored, said, "Tommy's an agent and lawyer for the guy who holds the surfing world record." Her eyes beamed.

"Well, up until yesterday. Chaz previously held the world's record. The World Surf League awarded it to a 37-year-old Brazilian who rode an 80-foot wave in Portugal just yesterday. Up until then, we did have bragging rights. These events are held here in Florida in the springtime around the college breaks. We have camps for kids and a lot of events for the adults. You should come out. We'll be at Pass-A-Grille beach all weekend."

Kathy placed her hand in the center of Tommy's chest in a

possessive move that I couldn't miss. No way in hell she wanted me to visit the event and spend another second with Tommy.

"Let's go, darling. Molly has work to do." Kathy blinked continuously at me. "And I need to get a manicure."

The comment about a manicure didn't escape me. Hadn't she just been at the salon with Penny?

"Okay, good seeing you again," Tommy said to Granny and me. "Nice meeting you, Aurora."

"Come back any time," Aurora said.

Kathy smiled and then frowned. "But wait, we haven't told her our news!"

Tommy shook his head. "I'm an idiot. Mo, we…um…Kathy and I…wanted to let you know that we're engaged."

My heart sank, but it had no reason to. I hadn't seen or talked to Tommy in over three years. But hearing him say the words hurt. I was so shocked I barely remembered to respond. "That's…well, that's good news. Kathy told me when she came in yesterday."

Tommy glanced at his fiancée. Kathy held out her left hand, and my eyes widened at the ring she had flashed at me the day before. A large round diamond surrounded by a halo of smaller yellow diamonds sparkled in the café's bright lights.

"It's gorgeous." I gritted my teeth and took the high road. "Congratulations."

Kathy gave me an unnerving glare.

I wasn't worried about her.

At least not yet.

CHAPTER NINE

Once the café door shut, Aurora looked around to make sure no one was within hearing distance and leaned toward me.

"Well, weren't you little Ms. Hospitable."

"She's been in my café twice in the last few days, and both times she's ended on the floor." I grinned. "And that look on her face when she saw Tommy eyeing her on the floor—well, I haven't seen someone turn that red since last year's strawberry pie-eating contest. What else could I have hoped for?"

"Lightning to strike her?"

I nodded. "Because of the engagement thing?" I asked Aurora, grateful that Granny had retreated to the kitchen in pursuit of food.

"No, because she's a bitch who stole your boyfriend in college."

I smiled at Aurora and prayed she hadn't seen the look in my eyes when Tommy announced their engagement. "I have to admit it hurt, but that ship sailed years ago. So no, it didn't bother me, but I'm not going to throw them an engagement party." I never pegged Tommy to marry Kathy, but maybe he had changed.

"Are you still going snooping at the hotel?"

"Yeah, I thought I could ask around about what day Kathy got to town. I didn't want to start asking questions about the manicure in front of Tommy," I said in a low voice, afraid others might hear.

Aurora nodded. "If Kathy is out running errands with Tommy, now may be a good time."

"Okay, help me change into the Sea Patrol getup," I said, wondering if a day at my café was ever going to start normally.

————

With my fake blonde ponytail clipped under my hat, large dark sunglasses, and my sea turtle emblem stapled to my tan vest, I entered the hotel.

Perspiration dribbled at the base of my neck, where the blonde ponytail lay. The morning showers off the coast had left the air hot and humid, turning me into a sticky, steamy mess.

The day before, Kathy had mentioned that she was staying at the Bonaire. I was surprised and grateful to find the lobby of the Bonaire Seaside hotel empty. The hotel, situated on the beach, was one of the dozens lining Gulf Boulevard. The four miles of the sandy beach had plenty of cozy seaside motels with sunset bars and restaurants. I was surprised that Kathy and Tommy weren't staying at the more luxurious and iconic pink Don Cesar hotel down the street.

The Bonaire lobby, with its ivory clay tile flooring and the whitewashed walls, was bright and cheery.

The front desk took up the right half of the corner. It was empty. I glanced behind the counter, halfway expecting to see a pegboard with room keys dangling from hooks. A small sign perched on a silver easel on the Formica counter read, *Be Right Back*.

As I turned to take a seat in the lobby, I heard a soft clicking noise behind me. I turned to see the sound coming from the maid's cart as a short woman with her back to me rolled it down the hall and stopped in front of a room.

It was tempting to ask the housekeeper first if she'd seen Kathy, but I decided to wait until the front desk clerk returned from break.

After ten minutes, the clerk hadn't returned, but the house-keeping cart and its driver were back in the hallway.

I adjusted my fake ponytail and walked up to the woman.

Humming to herself, the housekeeper concentrated on filling her apron pockets with tiny bottles of shampoos and other toiletries.

I smiled and strolled casually toward her.

"Excuse me," I said.

She regarded me and smiled. Her name tag read *Alice*.

"Hi. Alice?" I asked.

She stared at me, curious but courteous. "Si, I mean, yes. Can I get you something? More towels?"

"No. I'm not a guest."

Alice wrinkled her brow. She was standing stiffly and had on a pressed white cotton dress, white apron, and white sneakers. The dress looked two sizes too large for her.

"I was wondering if you can do me a favor," I started. "I'm Mo – Moline. I had talked to someone, a young woman, who had spotted a sea turtle nest, and my boss wants me to make sure it gets marked properly." I tilted my head. "You know how bosses can be." I pointed to my not-so official-looking turtle emblem. "I wondered if you had seen her."

Luckily, for me, my Aunt Tammera was an accomplished

liar, and I'd learned from her when she had lived with me and my mom.

Alice slowly smiled and said, "What can I help with?"

"I spoke with her on the beach, and I thought she said she was a guest here. I need to follow up with her, and I didn't get her name. No one was at the front desk. Can you tell me if you've seen her?" I explained.

Alice shrugged. "I don't know."

"It would be helpful if I can talk to her again." I pulled my iPhone from my pocket and opened a photo I had saved from Kathy's Facebook page. "Do you know this lady?"

She leaned over to view my iPhone. There was apparent recognition on Alice's face as her large brown eyes widened. "Oh yes. She was with a man. But I don't know where she is. Maybe you can check with the front desk."

I switched to a photo of Tommy. "This man?"

Alice regarded me suspiciously then replied, "No."

No? "Are you sure?"

She nodded her head.

"Okay, I have to report something to my boss. They will be worried if I can't even follow up on the location of the nest." I rubbed my chin and slipped my iPhone back into my pocket.

"I don't know where sea turtles are at," Alice mumbled in a broken accent.

"Yes, I understand. Not you, but this lady I talked to. I was wondering when you saw her. What day? And what did the man look like? What was he wearing?"

Her unreadable gaze searched my face and then shifted to the front lobby down the hallway. "You can check the front desk or the Ocean Spray. Maybe they can help there."

The Ocean Spray was the motel directly south of the Bonaire. "Why the Ocean Spray?"

"My sister works there. I took her lunch a few days ago. I

saw this lady in the photo talking with a man. I remember her because she was somewhat out-of-place."

"Out-of-place?" And did she say *a few days ago*?

"A beautiful lady, I noticed she had on boots. They were sitting outside in the sand under an umbrella table. She looked uncomfortable in the heat. Her face was red, and she looked like she was ready to cry." Alice glanced down the hall at a couple carrying beach towels. "I need to get back to work."

"Yes. Thank you so much. You've been very helpful. You saved my butt."

Saved my butt? Wow. I enjoyed this role-playing while snooping. I could almost imagine a mean boss.

Alice nodded, turned to busy herself with the housekeeping cart, and started humming.

I walked back to the lobby. The front desk was still empty. I pushed open the door and turned to see Alice hurrying to catch up with me.

"Miss?"

"Yes?"

"I forgot to mention that you can ask John, the waiter next door at the beach bar. He may know how to reach her."

"Thanks." I had a thought. "Wait, let me show you something."

Alice glanced around, a worried look on her face.

"This will only take a second." I opened Google and typed in Jerry Ryder Mistack, reporter. I clicked on images, and a passport-looking photo came into focus.

"Is this the man that was with the lady?"

She stared down at the photo and nodded. "Si. That's him."

"Thanks. And it was two days ago that you saw them?"

"Yes."

"Thanks again." My head was whirling.

"Good luck," Alice said and scurried back into the lobby.

I shot her a glance, nodded, and turned back to the parking lot where I had left my Grandpa's ancient Oldsmobile.

I was just about to walk over to my car when my back stiffened as I turned toward the street and saw a Deputy cruiser pull in. I turned, and a long tail of blonde hair landed across my chest. I was about to fling it off me when I realized it was my wig and my red hair coverup, which meant Drew wouldn't recognize me from this distance.

Deputy Lucky opened the driver's door and was leaning against the patrol car as he adjusted his holster's belt. A smile softened his determined-looking face.

I hoped he wouldn't recognize me standing several yards away, watching him. He was so darn cute, but there was no way he could see me here, especially asking questions about Kathy and the dead man.

I had to sneak away before he recognized me. If I'd been inside the hotel, I could have exited through the back lobby and on to the beach. I could walk the shoreline to the Ocean Spray. But it was too late to go back in. We would both be walking side-by-side, and even though I had a wig on, he'd recognize me.

On my right was a tiki hut in the corner of the parking lot for Segway rentals and tours, and several tourists were milling around. Drew was to my left. I scanned the palm tree-lined street, checking to see if I could exit another way. The Segway tiki hut was my only option.

I lowered my head and walked briskly toward the small thatched roof structure. When I reached it, I looked behind me. Drew was gone.

"Can I help you?" a voice said from behind the palm frond-lined counter.

"Um, yes. Hold on." I turned to see if I could make it to my car, but at that moment, I saw Drew through the lobby doors talking to the maid!

"Is it too late to join this tour?" I asked, pointing at a group of four or five tourists lined up on Segways.

"You're in luck. We have one spot left."

"Great." I reached into my vest pocket and pulled out my credit card.

"Read this and sign here," the tiki hut assistant said.

I perused the disclaimers and glanced at the rules and how-tos and then signed. A quick glance at the hotel confirmed Drew was still standing in the lobby chatting.

How long would I need to be away? I wondered. In the dead of Easter break, this tour could take up to forty-five minutes, as tourists and college kids crammed the streets walking, biking, scootering, and skateboarding.

"Remember to stay with the tour guide—" the instructor was saying, as he handed me a helmet. "You may want to remove your hat to get the helmet on."

Uh-oh. If I removed my cap, my hair came with it. And my red hair would get Drew's attention.

"I'm fine. I need to wear it for sun protection."

He eyed me suspiciously and then shrugged. "Then take this larger helmet and loosen the straps. It's adjustable."

I fiddled with the helmet and slid it over the cap.

"Do you think it would be okay if I stopped briefly at the Ocean Spray hotel on this thing? I have a friend there I need to talk to," I said.

"If you make it quick, we can stop there on our way back for a water break."

"Thank you." I felt sweat building on my head under my two layers of a cap and a helmet.

After a list of instructions, we were on our way. It crossed my mind that Deputy Lucky might recognize the Olds, so I glanced back at the motel. When I did, I spotted Drew walking out of the lobby, his eyes searching up and down the parking lot. I tucked my head down and accelerated.

"Hey, watch where you're going," a fellow Segway driver said.

"Sorry." I looked behind me and saw Drew return to the lobby.

————

Thirty minutes later, I was a sweaty mess. We had made a loop and were headed back to the Bonaire Seaside Motel. The weight of the helmet had managed to force the staples in the fake pony-tail into my scalp. I felt sure I'd have blood and sweat running down my back if I didn't stop.

Fortunately, I could see the Ocean Spray hotel on my left a few yards up the sidewalk.

Unfortunately, I couldn't see the small dog that shot out in front of me as I attempted to make a left into the hotel parking lot.

I panicked, and instead of braking, I accelerated. Suddenly I was one of the Dukes of Hazard on a Segway. If it weren't for the neat row of hibiscus hedges, I would have kept right on flying through the parking lot.

The dog owner, carrying a beach bag and neon pink raft, chased after the pup. She screamed when she saw me headed their way.

The Segway was hard to control. Involuntarily, I finally managed to brake, and the Segway went into a long slide, cutting a wide arc across the sidewalk. While playing Dale Earhart, Jr. on two wheels, I saw a Deputy car turn the corner. I swerved to the right, jumped the curb, and slammed the Segway into a hibiscus bush as tall as a garage. I felt the helmet slip from my head, and I thought for certain I'd need a skin graft where the ponytail ripped part of my scalp.

The dog lady carrying her beach bag had jumped out of my way. She went flying, scattering towels, suntan lotion, and the rubber raft in all directions.

Gingerly, I sat up, pulling a stray bunch of hibiscus flowers from my hair.

My hair? Since the helmet had popped off, my bright red frizzy hair was now exposed. The fresh breeze I felt on my head was my sweaty scalp sans the helmet, cap, and ponytail. I frantically looked around but didn't find the fake hair.

"Are you all right?" I asked the lady.

"Yes, are you?" she said, eyeing me.

"I'm fine," I said, standing up. "So sorry."

"What in God's name were you thinking?" a familiar voice said.

I whirled around to see Deputy Drew standing behind me with his hands on his hips.

"Um, I —" This was going to be a tough one to lie my way out of.

He leaned over and tugged at the cuff of his khaki pants.

"I suppose this stapled-on hair belongs to you?"

The blonde ponytail with a mess of silver staples seemed to be stuck to his pant leg. He tried to shake it loose.

"Not sure what you're talking about," I replied. I quickly put my hand across my chest, hoping he didn't see the sea turtle emblem.

"Uh-huh. And I'm supposed to believe you're just out for a joy ride in the middle of the week instead of working."

"Yes. Is it illegal to take the afternoon off here?"

Deputy Drew had a bad habit of giving me a citation or threatening to write me a ticket every time he turned around.

Half the time, I didn't deserve them, but other times were questionable.

"No, it's not illegal. We do allow vacations to our local residents. But it is illegal to park a Segway in a hibiscus bush."

I thought Drew might laugh at me. Or at the very least find my faux pas amusing, but when I looked up at him, he was not laughing. He wasn't even smiling. "Um, the dog ran out in front of me, and well, your timing sucks. If you're going to write me a ticket, let's get on with it. It's steamy hot out here." I brushed my matted hair from my face. I bent down to upright the Segway.

"Here, let me help you with that." Drew leaned over and grabbed the handlebars.

I looked around and noticed the dog lady and her unleased pup had left the scene. Several of the pedestrians who had stopped to watch continued walking once they realized no one was hurt or being arrested. I was just about to suggest I take the Segway back to the tiki hut when the guide showed up with another rider.

"Let us take this back," he said. "Can you get to your car from here?"

"Yes. Sorry about the crash. It seems good," I said, pointing at the Segway.

The guide and his rider hopped off his Segway and looked at me then Drew. "No problems, officer. We have insurance and any damage done to the bushes we can repair."

What was I, chopped liver?

"You can take that up with the hotel. I'll see to it that Ms. Brewster makes it back to her vehicle safely," Drew said.

Now I was Ms. Brewster, not Molly?

The Segway guide picked up my helmet, jumped on my Segway, and his rider took the other Segway. "Thanks for doing business with us. Please leave a five-star review on Yelp," he said and took off.

Drew turned back to me. "You weren't asking questions around the motel, were you? I don't want to find out that you're interfering with my murder investigation."

"So are you saying you have a suspect staying at the hotel?" I asked.

Drew narrowed his eyes. "I didn't say that."

"Then what are you doing here?"

"I'm the cop. I'll ask the questions."

"Okay, ask."

"I'm wondering what you're doing here."

"As I said, I was taking a tour. I've always wanted to know more about the beaches and the area."

"Did you learn anything?"

Was he talking about the beach area? Or my questioning at the hotel?

To be safe, I'd have to assume he was asking about what I learned on the tour and not from the maid.

"I learned that Silas Dent was one of the first inhabitants of our island. He was a hermit and lived in a shack all year, but every Christmas, he came to the beach and acted like Santa Claus. With his long white bread, he would sit at the beach and hand out presents to all the kids."

"Uh-huh." He nodded. "That's what you learned?"

"Yup."

Drew closed his eyes for a second like he was mentally counting to ten and then inhaled.

"What's that?" He pointed to the sea turtle emblem, now peeling off my vest.

I didn't know what to say. "Look, unless it's illegal to wear a shirt supporting sea turtles, then I say we should be talking about dinner plans for tonight versus my choice of clothing."

He gave my outfit one more look-over, then sighed and shook his head.

"Do you need a ride back to the Olds?"

So that confirmed Drew knew I was at the Seaside hotel earlier. And was I supposed to believe he coincidentally showed up at the Ocean Spray motel just when I returned from the tour? Was there anything he didn't know?

"Thank you, but I can walk."

His cell phone chimed. He removed it from his pocket and read a text. He frowned. "I've got to run. Do you want to meet at Granny's around five to look at the Sea Ray?"

"Yes. That'll work. I'll have Henrietta set another place at the table."

"I don't want to impose."

"It's lasagna night."

"Okay then, it's a date." He smiled and kissed my cheek. I felt my face flush.

Before walking away, he turned around and handed me the ponytail.

"You won't be needing this anymore." He winked.

CHAPTER TEN

I was still cursing to myself over the Segway crash as I walked through the parking lot of the Bonaire Seaside Motel. The Oldsmobile was a few steps in front of me. I kept my head down in fear of the Segway owner and his team spotting me. I'd had enough embarrassment for one day.

It should have been a cakewalk getting to my car unnoticed, but then I didn't expect to see Kathy!

She was standing close to the tiki hut talking to a tall man who wasn't Tommy. I wanted to speak to Kathy, but I debated whether my appearance would seem too suspicious.

One glance back at the hotel showed no signs of Tommy and another survey of the parking lot showed no signs of Drew's police cruiser. Then I remembered Drew had gotten a call. What was the call he had responded to that made him leave so quickly? Police matters?

While Kathy looked to be in deep conversation with the man, I resisted the urge to jump in my car. I could have left without being seen and gone home and taken a long bath and then a nap. But after all, I had come here to talk to Kathy, and despite Drew's warnings, I was going to do it.

I strolled up to Kathy and interrupted her and the man, who was in a meaningless discussion about the previous night's sunset on the Gulf.

"I took ten photos with my iPhone. They were spectacular," Kathy said in a flirty voice, with her back to me.

"Kathy, is that you?" I asked, feigning surprise.

She turned, and at first her expression was sour, but then she remembered her manners, and she smiled warmly at me. "Molly, what are you doing here?"

I shrugged. "I volunteer for sea turtle patrol now and then." I might as well keep up the charade.

She looked at my autumn-toned outfit with the torn emblem, and a small disapproving grin formed. She had on yet another colorful sundress with matching espadrilles and purse, and she looked straight out of the Lilly Pulitzer catalog.

The tall man turned to join a few others before she could introduce him. Darn!

"Well, aren't you being so charitable helping out the sea life? Why are you here?" Kathy asked, still eyeing my clothes with suspicion.

"Someone spotted a turtle nest and I was here to—"

"Well, well, well, if it isn't the hibiscus hedge-killer," a voice said from behind me.

I turned around to see the Segway manager.

Kathy's eyebrows lifted.

"Hey, sorry about that," I said to the man.

I glanced at the sky that was suddenly full of clouds preparing for the late-afternoon spring showers. We had time for a quick drink. *Why not?* I thought. Then I turned to Kathy. "Do you want to grab a cold beer or something on the beach?"

She hesitated but then nodded.

"There's Sandbar Bill's out back. It's a patio bar," I said. "Let's meet there in two minutes. I have one thing to do."

"I can wait. And please tell me you're going to change. And maybe run a brush through your hair."

"Sorry, this is all I have. I didn't realize it was National Wear Your Lilly Day."

"You know Molly, I actually miss this. It's been a long time since I had a friend who could tell me what she thought. I'll go grab a table." Kathy actually smiled as she turned and strolled toward the hotel.

"Thanks, I'll be there a minute. Order me a rum runner with extra cherries."

"Two rum runners it is."

I watched Kathy leave and then turned toward the tiki. I planned to pay for the bush repair and snap a picture of the man Kathy had been talking to about sunsets. As I pulled out my iPhone, I wondered what the going rate for hibiscus bushes was.

———

It had been a painful catching up session with Kathy. We'd been sitting at the seaside patio restaurant for over twenty minutes. She was on her second rum runner, and I had barely three gulps of mine. Dang, they were sweet juice drinks. And powerful. They had Kathy rambling on and on.

Suddenly, there was shouting from the beach.

"What are you doing? It was my turn to serve," a teenage girl yelled at her friend. Both girls were playing two-man volleyball against two guys.

"That looks familiar," Kathy commented.

We both had played volleyball growing up and could beat any amateur pair.

"Yeah, we could beat the best."

"Whatever happened to us?"

I felt a slight blush of pink color my cheeks, but I wasn't

going to admit how much those teenage girls reminded me of Kathy and me not too many years ago.

"You really want to go there?"

"Oh hell, you and Tom were over way before he and I started dating."

She may have had something there, but Kathy had pushed him over the edge. I always felt Tommy had left me knowing that another person was waiting for him when he was single. That was Kathy. But then, I always wondered if she hadn't been the one there for him, maybe there would have been another woman close behind.

"I really don't see any reason to go through all this," she said. "You're right; this chance meeting is not going to be…" Kathy's voice trailed off as she glanced around and then buried herself into her drink.

I contemplated my next comment. Maybe Kathy was right. "I didn't expect us to ever be having a drink together. Not like this." Uncertainty clogged my brain.

"It's not a big deal." She turned, wincing a little, as we both watched a young mother wrap a towel around her daughter's shoulders and usher her gently back to the shade of an umbrella.

It was Kathy's grin that made me wonder. No more than that.

"Thanks for talking and having a drink with me," Kathy said. "I don't have too many friends, especially around here. People always judge me based on their perception of me."

What perception? That you're a backstabbing, conniving bitch who steals her best friend's boyfriend? That's what I really wanted to say, but I was here to get answers, so instead, I said, "Well, we had our issues in the past, but we're beyond that now."

"Thanks. I know what you and everyone think. I mean, look

at me. I can't help it if I like fancy things, and that I used to be a model."

I struggled to keep my eyes from rolling up into my head at Kathy's pretentiousness. My first-grade teacher used to tell me eye-rolling was not acceptable.

"You were eleven when you modeled. You hadn't even reached puberty. We were all cute before that."

"Well, it started me on the right path."

"Your mom started you down that path, Kathy. You can choose to be whomever you want now."

"I know." She took a gulp of her drink nervously, then said, "He likes everything. Cupcakes, cookies, and now supposedly cats."

Was this conversation going to be about her and Tommy's relationship?

"But you've known Tommy a long time. He couldn't have changed that much." But I had to admit Tommy used to be all about his health and weight. He never ate sweets, and he worked out all the time. And I knew he had been a dog lover and never had mentioned cats.

She looked at me and shrugged. "I guess you're right. He just seems different now that we're engaged."

"Different?"

"He seems," Kathy hesitated, "unstable."

I motioned for her to go on, afraid to comment.

Kathy twirled the pink paper umbrella between her fingers. It left a gooey residue on her thumb and forefinger. She was clearly unraveled about something. What could Tommy be doing that would leave this polished woman frustrated enough to have a drink with his ex-girlfriend and stain her fingers with cherry juice?

She told me about a discussion about the wedding and how

they were planning a cake tasting one day. He had shown up late.

"He was a mess," she said.

I observed Kathy's eyes through her lightly tinted Maui Jim sunglasses. Her eyes looked red and puffy.

"How so?" I asked without meddling too much. I knew Kathy was like a dormant volcano. It was only a matter of time before she blew.

"I think he's gambling."

"Gambling? You live in Oregon. Isn't it illegal there?" I was bewildered by Tommy's new love for sweets, but I found this accusation really out of character.

"He plays online," Kathy said.

Why was she sharing this with me? We used to be friends, but that ended when she and Tommy started a relationship. Something had to really be bothering Kathy for her to tell me intimate things about my ex-boyfriend.

"Want my opinion?"

"I'm afraid you're going to give it to me whether I like it or not." She swallowed the last bit of her drink and signaled to the waiter to bring her another. I was still nursing my first one.

"Confront him."

"But I'm afraid that it may be true," she replied. There was genuine concern, maybe even fear, in her tone. "Plus I have secrets of my own."

We sat there in silence for a few minutes while our waiter returned with a drink. He placed it in front of Kathy, a big smile on his face.

Kathy resumed explaining Tommy's odd behavior lately.

I smiled and nodded politely.

I had to admit, Kathy could be on to something. But I wasn't here to be a marriage counselor for my two exes. I had to say, however, it made me warm inside that the two were starting out on a shaky path. A zebra doesn't change its stripes. And as much as I hated to tell Kathy, I believed that Tommy might be spending his money on a new woman and not online gambling. But I'd let her figure that out.

Kathy went on and on, and the redness in her cheeks and complexion made her appear as if the rum runners were kicking her butt.

After a pause in her litany of things about Tommy that concerned her, I found it an opportune time to ask about the murder victim. I wanted to see what her involvement was and to clear Penny's name.

"I guess you heard that reporter died."

"Who?"

"Don't act like you haven't met him. I know you're the one Penny saw talking to him at the park yesterday." *And at the hotel the day before, when you supposedly weren't even in town,* I thought.

"Who's Penny?"

"Oh, come on, Kathy. Don't act like you don't know Penny Jackson. You two got a pedicure at Island Salon."

"I really don't know what's gotten into you, Molly Brewster, but I can tell you I do not know Penny, and I certainly didn't have a nail appointment with her."

Boy, Kathy was good. She was either telling the truth, or she had gotten really good at lying.

If she really didn't know Penny, then who was the person spotted in the park? I tried a blunt inquiry. "Did you know Jerry?"

"Is he the reporter?"

"Jerry Ryder, but he goes by Jerry R. Mistack. An investigative reporter for the Herald. He writes human interest stories, with an emphasis on the business and hidden stories."

I didn't think it was possible, but Kathy's face turned an even brighter shade of red.

"By your reaction, I take it you knew him?"

She nodded and bit her lower lip.

I asked her again about her knowing Jerry.

"I had heard he was truly an awful person. No one liked him. He pissed off a lot of people. I'm not surprised someone knocked him off," she said.

"Did he come here to talk to you?"

Kathy began to cry. "I don't care about that reporter. I'm just upset about Tommy. And I know that Jerry guy said all those things about my family. He was just plain mean." She hiccupped and then took a sip of the fresh orange drink still sporting the paper umbrella.

I sat there, puzzled. What was I to say? Or should I let her cry or what? And who was mean? Tommy or the reporter?

"Are you okay?" I asked against my better judgment.

She sniffled and dabbed at her eyes with a paper napkin. "I'm fine. I don't know why you care about the reporter anyway."

"I can't help myself getting involved in detective work. If you know anything, you need to talk to Deputy Lucky."

"Who?" she asked, clearly not that upset over the reporter because the tears stopped quicker than they had started.

"Deputy Drew Powell."

"Oh yes, your boyfriend. I've already spoken to him."

I nodded woodenly. Deputy Drew was a few steps ahead of me. That didn't surprise me. What surprised me was that he had already figured out Kathy's presence in the park that day. But why did she deny she had been there?

Kathy tried adamantly to explain her family's relationship with the victim. "Yes, he had written derogatory articles about my brother over the years, and he and Cary squabbled over it.

But they weren't enemies. Cary didn't even give it a second thought, I assure you." Her face continued to redden as she defended her family.

"What about you?"

"What about me?"

"Did you ever confront Jerry about it?" I thought about what the housekeeper had said. That she had identified Kathy with Jerry. Wouldn't she want to keep her brother Cary and his family safe and sound from the harmful business accusations?

Before she could answer, Kathy's phone rang, and Kathy placed her enormous handbag on the table where I could see the contents. She rummaged through it, and I caught a glimpse of gloves.

Gloves?

Next to the pair of gloves, I saw a stack of index cards with newspaper articles taped to them. The reporter for the article was Jerry. What I read briefly on the paper made my jaw fall open.

"What's that?" I asked, pointing to the brown leather gloves.

Kathy flinched. She seemed to think about it for a moment before she answered. "Driving gloves. My hands get chapped."

"Don't your hands get sweaty?"

She swallowed. "They're kidskin, so they're lightweight. Sweat is better than red, chapped hands."

"Or good for covering up fingerprints," I retorted.

Kathy let out a sharp, bitter laugh. "Good try, Sherlock," she said. "You know, your deputy boyfriend has you doing all the sleuthing. Is this what the drinks are really all about?"

What could I say? The truth was I did want drinks with my ex-friend to determine her involvement in a recent murder. But I couldn't agree with her and have my whole house of cards fall down.

I sighed. "I never planned this get-together." That was the

truth.

She sat back against her seat, aghast. "But you want answers."

Kathy's cell phone buzzed again, and she glanced down at it, then she looked around, nervous and uncomfortable.

She began talking about her family.

As I sat and watched her, I felt excitement about the contents of Kathy's purse. Even as she chatted away, I worked through what I knew about the case. And it started to make sense. I began to think I was getting good at this sleuthing stuff.

Kathy was talking about her older brother when I felt a light tap on my shoulder. I whirled my head around to see Tommy.

He was wearing surfing trunks and a tank top and holding a skimboard. If he had been adding sweets to his diet, his physique didn't show it. Not an ounce of fat on him. Geez, he was really cute, and wowsa, much broader shoulders and tanner than I remembered. The blush that formed on my cheeks was automatic.

"What are you two doing here?" he said, puzzled.

Kathy looked apologetically at Tommy. "Um, we're just catching up."

Damn my luck. We had been interrupted before Kathy could finish. And just when I was gathering crucial information.

Tommy slammed the small board down next to our table hard enough to make the rum runners splash out of our glasses. Then he exploded with a few profanities.

"I tried texting and calling you. What in the world are you thinking, Kathy?" he yelled.

Half the people sitting near us turned to scrutinize us. I saw our waiter taking it all in.

"I really should be going," I said. I reached in my pocket and pulled out a twenty and laid it on the table. There was no use staying now. Kathy wouldn't talk with Tommy there. I had to get more answers, but I couldn't do it with an audience. I stood up to go.

In alarm, Kathy had pushed away from the table when Tommy laid into her.

She stuttered, "I need to go to the room. I feel a headache coming on. I need to rest up before dinner."

"No, you stay." Tommy forced Kathy back into her chair.

I stood there, puzzled. What was I to say? Or should I let them fight?

Kathy stayed silent too, like I had, still brooding about the dressing-down she received from Tommy.

"I'm sorry, Kathy, but I have to go. Granny needs me to run a few errands for her before I go back to the Bean."

Kathy sprang to her feet, away from Tommy. "I'll go with you to that salon, right? Tom, dear, you don't mind if I go get my nails manicured? They are such a mess," she said defensively before she could stop herself.

Tommy's head turned to me then Kathy; his eyes became instantly alert.

Kathy went on as if the two of us had been planning a trip to the nail salon all along. Why would she want to go with me and not stay with her fiancé? And why on earth would I plan a manicure with my ex-best friend? I didn't buy it. And from the looks of Tommy, he didn't either.

His anger flared. "No! You just had a manicure."

Busted. Kathy sank into her chair.

What was going on between these two? I said my goodbyes and turned away.

The whole scene was odd, to say the least, and my thoughts started to churn just as a few drops of rain hit my shoulder. I sprinted to the Olds, reenergized. I had no idea what was going on with those two.

But I was going to find out.

CHAPTER ELEVEN

If I had any doubt about getting information when I walked into the Island Salon, it soon changed. The turquoise walls and mermaid motif were relaxing and perfect for customers to spill their souls while getting their hair washed or their feet massaged.

I wondered if salon gossip was like the café gossip. Some of the stuff I had heard, you couldn't believe, but other things I had heard were close enough to the truth. I could easily change the name of my café from *Addicted to the Bean* to *Addicted to the Gossip*, and no one would even bat an eye.

"Molly!" Dana yelled as she came rushing over. "I knew you'd give in one day."

"No, I'm not here for a makeover," I replied.

"Nonsense. I have a special seat for you. Would you like coffee?"

"Um, yes, please." If I was to interrogate Dana or anyone else in the salon, I needed to kill the slight buzz from drinking a rum runner.

"Follow me." Dana led me to a small coffee bar. I creamed and sugared my coffee, then sat in Dawn's station.

"So…I can't help but notice your hair is lopsided. I've been wondering ever since you moved here when you would wander in for a style." Dana's sledgehammer of a hint was her way of trying to tell me my red-curly-mess-of-hair needed a professional touch versus the usual twenty-dollar trim I invested in every few months.

I grimaced at my disheveled image in the mirror. I shrugged. What the heck, why not?

"Do your magic, Dana."

———

Dana's hands moved fast as she blow-dried my hair. And her mouth moved faster. For the last twenty minutes, I had learned more gossip about Bay Isles and its denizens than I'd learn in a week at the café.

Dana turned off the dryer and swiveled the white leather chair to face the mirror. "So what do you think?"

My curls were gone and replaced by a tamer, slightly shorter, shoulder-length wavy bob.

"It's awesome. I can hardly believe that straightening my hair makes me look so—"

"So beautiful," Dana interrupted. "You're a pretty girl, Molly, and if you'd take care of yourself, you'd attract that on-again, off-again boyfriend of yours for good."

I scrunched up my eyebrows at her. I knew what she was doing. She wanted gossip on me and Drew! I wasn't biting and fueling her next conversation to some not-so-innocent gossip-hungry resident.

I glanced at the floor where snippets of half-moon curls of red hair had been flung all around the chair's silver base.

"How is Deputy Lucky?" Dana was relentless. She was not going to let this go.

I laughed and sighed, earning a glare from Dana.

"Well, if you must know, we are not on-again, off-again. We've been 'on' since the first of the year. He's just swamped, so we don't have enough time together to take the relationship to the next level." This was the truth. Anyone who knew us as a couple could surmise that much, including a nosy salon owner.

"Hmm," was all Dana replied.

I crossed my arms in front of me. "What does that mean?" I heard the accusation in my tone, but I squinted my eyes at her too.

"I've seen him out and about." Dana paused dramatically, balancing a teasing comb in her fingers. "That's all." She shrugged.

I stared at her carefully, just as a patient cat might watch a startled mouse. "About where? He lives ten miles away and works here as a beat cop, so of course you'd see him." Okay, so she had me rising to the bait.

"Well, it's probably nothing." Once again, the shrug.

Oh, here we go. I came here for answers, but now I have to listen to salon gossip about the guy I'm dating. "What's nothing?"

Dana reached her hand out and placed it on my shoulder. I thought it was a kind gesture until she took out her scissors and snipped at an imaginary fly-away strand. "I've seen him out on his boat."

"Drew does like fishing and boating. He may also be working a case—"

"— with a," she sighed, " a girl." Her voice turned calm.

My heart skipped a beat, while Dana lowered her head and said, "It may have been nothing, but I was out with Old Man Rob and his son Joey. He's been trying to hook me up with his Joey for twenty years now. Anyway, we had just dropped our lines into Mullet Bay when we heard the boat's engine. At first,

I didn't recognize the boat, but as it got closer, I recognized it was Drew's."

She held a hint of amusement in her face, as if she had successfully sprung a trap for me to be paralyzed in. All I could do now was sit and listen.

"Was it his police boat?" I asked, trying to sound nonchalant.

"No, his own boat. He wasn't in uniform."

I simply stared at her, no longer trusting my ability to talk with a watermelon-sized lump in my throat. Drew had only taken me out on his boat once since I'd know him.

I nodded, and my newly coiffed hair bobbed with me. It was a strange feeling. But everything about this day was strange. Drinks with my ex-best friend, her fight with my ex-college-boyfriend, and now my current boyfriend was seen boating with another woman.

Dana's constant barrage of chatter drifted in and out. She was giving me her opinion on me not wearing makeup.

She reached for my hand, and I shrank away.

"Come on, let me do your makeup. This way." Dana led me from the swivel chair. I was acutely aware of a few eyes on me. She led me back through the obstacle course of the shampoo basins and women propped under large dryers, to a less crowded, brightly lit makeup room. I tried to tune out the usual salon noises of customers chatting, water running, and phones ringing.

Dana settled me into a well-lit station in front of dozens of makeup compacts, brushes of all sizes, and lipsticks in many colors.

"All PETA-friendly. 100 percent cruelty-free," Dana said. "Animal by-products hide everywhere."

I didn't respond because I knew Dana was a vegan. And I

suspected she not only worried about what she put in her mouth but what she put on her body.

"Take it from me. Skip the animal ingredients. I know, disgusting. These are plant-based." She held up a jar with a black label with a "cruelty-free" logo.

I nodded

"Take your pick. Would you rather breathe in citrus or sludge? Up to you," she said.

"You're the boss." My mind was still swirling over Drew.

"Imagine seeing just one photo of a bunny with severe burns all over his body from product testing, and you'll be convinced. Trust me."

I nodded again. All I wanted was for her to finish, so I could get back to the Bean.

"Do you have a date with Deputy Lucky tonight?"

"No," I responded bluntly. "I mean, yes, he is coming to Granny's for dinner." We were going to look at Grandad's Sea Ray then eat with Granny and Henrietta.

"It's lasagna night." Why did I add that in? I wanted to hear more about Drew and the other woman on a boat ride.

"Henrietta makes the best lasagna."

"You've had it?"

"Of course." Dana picked up a brush, dabbed it in tan cream makeup, and started contouring my face. I felt like a porcelain easel.

"Henrietta brought us lasagna when Dad had his hip surgery."

I nodded.

"Do you moisturize?" she asked.

"What?"

"Never mind." Dana laughed. "I'll just add a little more concealer under your eyes to take away the puffiness."

Dana's pink-nailed hand held a small brush. "Look up. That's it."

Dana's face was so close to mine that while she dabbed the cream under my eyes, I could smell the peppermint in her mouth. And before I could warn her, I recoiled and sneezed.

"Ah-choo! Ah-choo!"

"Gawd bless you," Dana said.

"Thanks, it's the peppermint," I managed to squeeze in before the third, "Ah-choo!"

I heard a few *Gesundheits* come from the front room. I replied with *thank you*.

"Aw, yes. You have that allergy." Dana reached over and pulled out two Kleenexes from a box. She handed one to me and used the other to spit her peppermint into. She tossed the tissue in the trash, and after I wiped my nose, I did the same.

She went back to applying more makeup, but when she spoke, she drew back away from my face. "Look, that boat thing with Drew—I'm sure they were working on a case or something."

"Oh yeah, there are several woman detectives in the neighboring towns. What did she look like?"

"Tall blonde." Dana paused, holding an eyelash curler. "From what I could see." Her brown eyes widened, and her pointy chin gave her a mysterious, almost evil look. "Come to think of it, she probably was a detective, but I don't think she was from around here."

"Why do you say that?"

"There was something odd about her."

"Odd?"

"She wore brown boots."

"Boots on a boat?"

Dana grinned and nodded. "Weird, huh?"

"Like rubber boots? Like fishing boots?" I owned a pair of

rubber Hunter boots. I always felt official and waterproof when I wore them, even if they were sky blue with red roses on them.

"No, like cowboy boots." When she said *cowboy*, she let her voice lapse into a Southern drawl.

Oh no! Would he have taken Kathy out? What were the odds that two women wore cowboy boots in the Florida sunshine?

I had to keep down the bile building in the back of my throat.

"Are you okay, Molly?" Dana asked.

I nodded and panted, "Do you have more details about her? It's just that he's working all these cases, and I'm trying to help out."

"We were so far away. I don't think he even saw us, because we waved, but he turned and didn't wave back." The last comment was punctuated with a few pats of an itchy makeup brush.

She stepped back and sighed with satisfaction at the excellent job she had done on me.

I was thankful she had covered my cheeks with a dark pink dusting of blush because my own skin was turning fifty shades of red.

———

In the last ten minutes, I had managed to pay for my salon services, get outside, and turned my shaky legs on the sidewalk, and fled. I had been walking in the direction of the Bean. I wanted to sneak in the back door and lock myself in my office and think. And breathe.

The fresh air did me good.

When I reached my café, I walked around the boardwalk, managing to avoid seeing anyone. I popped in the back door and went straight to my tiny office.

Within seconds, Aurora was in the office. "I saw you sneak in," she began. "Woo, woo, check out the new Molly Brewster. You look gorgeous, I mean absolutely gorgeous, and so made-up."

I didn't reply. I was too busy trying to fight off my tears of emotion.

"Look at you." Aurora paused, then she realized I wasn't smiling.

"What is it? What's wrong?" Aurora asked, seeing my puffy eyes.

I was afraid I was going to throw up or pass out. I panted.

"Mo, breathe."

"I am breathing," I said.

"No, I think you're hyperventilating."

I drew in a deep breath and turned to run to the bathroom.

Aurora followed me. And watched as I did exactly what I'd been afraid of. I heaved over the toilet and spilled my rum runner and the contents of my stomach into the tiny porcelain bowl. Then I crumpled next to it and burst into tears.

Aurora flushed the toilet, then dampened a paper towel and handed it to me. She retrieved another one and placed the cold rag under my hair at the nape of my neck.

"Not the reaction you expected?" I finally said as I turned to my dear friend.

She shook her head, and a small smile flitted over her lips.

I thought about how ridiculous I must look. All made up with my head buried in the toilet.

I smiled. And before I knew it, we both started laughing.

"What in the world, Mo?" Aurora finally said, collapsing on the cold tile floor next to me.

I sat up straighter. Where did I begin?

———

Aurora slumped in the kitchen chair and reached for another iced cupcake.

"I mean, maybe he is training a new detective," she said between bites of the gooey cherry vanilla cupcake.

I nodded, still picking at the half-eaten white and pink cupcake on my plate.

"Remember what's-her-name last year?" Aurora offered.

"Detective Lacey?"

"Yes, the lady of steel."

"But why were they on his personal boat?"

"They were undercover. You said yourself he is investigating the boat thieves. And maybe that's why he didn't wave at Dana."

I felt distinctly lightheaded still, so I forced a few bites of the cupcake in my mouth.

"It could mean a lot of things. But I hate that Drew can't share it with me."

"I heard it's tough being a detective's significant other. They are sworn not to talk about their cases. And besides, you're always snooping."

"But in a good way. I've helped solve a few crimes around here."

"That you have. So let's get a plan of action. Get out your moleskin; let's see what you have already."

I sighed. "You know me too well, Aurora."

I reached for my backpack and pulled out my red notebook. I flipped to the last page with entries on it.

I consulted my list. I had names across the top: Kathy, Penny, Dana, Tommy, mystery woman... under the names was a list of questions.

"Well," said Aurora, leaning over my notebook, "I know you've talked to Kathy and Dana, and indirectly Tommy. What about visiting Penny?"

"She won't talk to me again."

"Then I'll do it," Aurora said. She picked up a perfectly decorated cupcake and stared at it.

"I'll deliver her baked goods."

"What will you do?" Granny's voice came from the kitchen door. I turned around to see Granny and Henrietta trailing her.

Both women murmured with awe at the sight of my new coiffed look.

"Well, if it isn't about time," Granny said.

Henrietta beamed.

"No comment. I needed to talk to Dana," I said.

"About the polish?" Henrietta said.

Suddenly I remembered Dana's words about Drew and the mysterious woman on the boat, and my heart sank again.

"Look, I need to go home and feed Kona. Can we meet at my house in 15 minutes?" I asked the three women in my tiny café kitchen.

They all stared at me.

"What about lasagna?" Henrietta asked.

"Drew just texted me. He can't make it to dinner tonight. Something's come up."

"Let me put some sandwiches together then," Granny said.

"We'll see you in a few."

I was out the back door racing to my apartment before anyone could object.

CHAPTER TWELVE

Three of the most important people in my life sat around my kitchen table. Granny, Aurora, and Henrietta were sipping iced tea. Snickers lay at my feet and Kona was on my lap. My moleskin and laptop were open and ready for use.

"Who would want Jerry dead?" I thought about the most critical elements of any crime.

I wrote down a few items in my red moleskin: *Motive, Suspects, Facts.*

"From what I've heard, a lot of people didn't like the stories he wrote about them," Granny said.

"But would the bad press be enough of a motive?" Aurora asked, squirming more than usual in the chair.

"It's a start. If we knew what he reported on in the last year, we could rule out any of the articles," I said.

"What about his ex-wife? I heard she hated him," Aurora said.

"That's speculative. We need hard facts."

"Well, we don't have any."

"On the contrary. We know that he was in town to do an

article on Bay Isles. We know he was killed with a serrated kitchen knife that came from Mary Dedham's strawberry pie."

"Technically, according to Drew, they don't think the knife killed him. And the clunk on his head came from something heavy," I added.

"What?" Granny asked.

I rubbed my chin. I recalled the image I saw of Jerry when the paramedics had covered the body. Should I explain my theory now? I still had some research to do. "Let's just say I have a hunch what the murder weapon could be, and it was heavy, but it wasn't a rock. And the murderer took it with him."

"Or her," Henrietta said.

"Or her." I nodded at Henrietta.

"Can you tell us what you think it could be?" Granny asked.

"I saw the grass around where the body was found. Something had been dragged through the brush from the sandy beach. It left distinctive marks. Some I'm very familiar with when I go boating." I looked at Aurora. "Oh, come on. Heavy. Dragged to shore. At the beach…"

Three sets of eyes on me, blank stares.

"The marks in the sand around the body. At first, I thought they were from Gucci's leash, but they were too deep. And then I figured it out when I watched people boating, and they anchored off Bunces Pass," I said.

"And?" Granny asked.

"And it was windy, so most boats had to use the bow and the aft anchors."

"Okay?" Aurora said.

"An anchor!" Granny yelled.

I nodded. "That's what I suspect."

"So it would have to be someone who could easily carry an anchor around," Aurora said.

"Good point. How much do they weigh?" Henrietta asked.

"A Fortress is light," I said. "We have one in Granddad's boat. I plan to take my paddleboard out late at night and approach the park from the beach. I'll walk the path directly to where the vic was found and look for clues. I need to check out the water bottom in that area that day. If it was an anchor, the type of water bottom, whether mud, sand, grasses, or coral or rock, could dictate the type of anchor used."

"Can we rule out a female if it was a heavy anchor swung at Jerry?" Aurora asked.

"Not quite yet," I said. "But carrying an anchor would indicate it was a light one."

"Or a strong back and arms," Granny added. "I know I couldn't carry one far."

"But you're old," I said, grinning at Granny.

"So we can rule out old people?" Henrietta murmured.

"Sure. But you'd be surprised. Our Fortress anchor is made of aluminum, and even though it only weighs 21 pounds, it can sustain a 5,000-pound load." I smiled.

"Someone's been doing her research," Aurora said.

"Some of these small bullet points that are on my list, I'll be able to check off after I survey the area by paddleboard." I made a checkmark next to the murder weapon.

"What else do you have?" Granny asked, putting on her glasses and leaning over my notebook. "What do the boat thieves have to do with it? And what's this drawing of a bunny here for?"

"I'm not sure if the boat thieves have anything to do with Jerry's murder or not." I stood up to grab the pitcher of sweet tea to refill everyone's glasses.

"I had a drawing of a bunny to remind myself to ask the park rangers if they have an abundance of rabbits there," I said from the refrigerator.

I walked back to the table. "Typically, that close to water, there aren't many rabbits due to the alligators and lack of grasses for them to eat."

Before I could pour tea in the glasses, Henrietta grabbed the pitcher from me and walked around, refilling and draining the pitcher.

"What am I missing?" Henrietta asked as she filled my glass with the last of the tea.

"Penny said she had to use the steak knife to cut Gucci's leash because her dog chased a bunny," Aurora said.

"You think she's lying?" Henrietta asked.

"We're just trying to find answers."

"Who do you have as suspects?" Granny asked.

"So far, I have Penny, Kathy, mystery woman at the park, and that's about it."

"All women," Granny said. "What about you?"

"Me?" I replied, a bit taken aback by Granny's comment.

"You did argue with Jerry and ended up going to the police station because you punched him. But I'm only kidding. I know you had nothing to do with it, but the police may be suspicious of that event too."

"I told you all, and like I told the new Deputy Cross, Jerry pinched me, so I clobbered him with a basket full of eggs."

"That's a little egg...stravagant. Isn't it?" Aurora laughed at her play on words.

"That's murder with an eggs...clamation point," Granny added.

"Okay, enough of the jokes." I grinned.

"There's no egg...scaping it," Aurora said.

We all started laughing, and Snickers barked, and Kona meowed.

"Eggs...actly!" I loved my friends I had made in my new home.

"Let's get back to our list. We know that Penny found the body," Granny finally said.

"Aurora is going to Penny's house to take her sweets. Aurora will ask her questions and maybe talk to her husband," I said.

"We don't have a lot of suspects. Do the police have a suspect?" Granny asked me.

"I don't think so."

"Do you think Penny could have done it?" Aurora asked. "Do the police think she's a suspect?"

"I heard the police have been interviewing Penny and her neighbors," Henrietta said.

"If Penny is all they have, then I'm worried about our police force," Granny commented.

"Why?"

"Well, she may be a bitch, sometimes–" Granny started to say.

"Granny," I warned.

"Penny Jackson can get on everyone's nerves. But she loves her children and as stuck-up as she is, I don't see her as a murderer. Besides, she does so much for this community."

"I have to agree. She's not the most likable person," I added to Granny's comment.

"But she has principles. And her family is very grounded in Bay Isles. I've known her parents and grandparents for years," Granny said.

"But she did find the body," I said.

"You, of all people, should know that means nothing."

Granny was right. I had found a body on the beach a few months earlier, and that and other evidence placed me as the number one suspect. I had nothing to do with the murder but being a suspect had driven me to help the local authorities find the real killer. My allergy to peppermint helped solve the crime. Well, that, and my nosy hunches.

In complete agreement, I nodded and said, "Let's leave her on the list for now, until Aurora visits her."

"I had a drink with Kathy," I finally told my close group of friends.

There were several blank stares.

"I know you're a risk-taker, but you're not stupid," Granny said.

"I'd already spent half of my day impersonating a sea life volunteer. I didn't think impersonating a friend of Kathy's would be that much harder." I explained how I had accidentally run into her and how the rum runners were making her talk until we were interrupted by Tom.

"I guess with all your shenanigans on the Segway and the bushes, having a drink with your ex-best friend could hardly be considered a crime," Granny murmured.

"Did she recognize you with the blonde hair extensions?" Aurora asked.

"Oh, I lost those in my run-in with the bushes." I went on to tell them about Tommy's outburst at Kathy.

"What an odd but productive day," Aurora smiled.

"To say the least. I thought when I moved to Bay Isles, my biggest fear would be I'd be bored to death," I said. "Instead, in only a few months, I've managed to be a suspect in a murder case, solved that same murder, be molested while wearing a bunny costume, involved in another murder case, and now I'm stalking my ex-boyfriend and his new fiancée."

"If that's the worst that has happened to you, then I'd say you're ahead of the game," Aurora said.

"Well, a good distraction now and then does one good," Granny said.

"What about Kathy? Do you really think she's a suspect?

She does have a crappy attitude, but I didn't take her for a killer. Unless she fooled me," Henrietta said.

"A mosquito with a lobotomy could fool you," Granny replied.

I sneered at Granny and smiled at Henrietta. "I agree. She has a motive, with the reporter's connection to her brother, but she doesn't seem the murdering type."

"She has the resources. She could have easily rented a small boat," Aurora paused, "with a Fortress or lightweight anchor. And when she anchored on shore, she could have lured the reporter toward her."

"Maybe she was wearing a sexy bathing suit—you know, those French numbers with her bare cheeks hanging out," Henrietta added.

"And then she tells him she has engine issues. He follows her into the brush to get to her boat, and she clobbers him," Granny said.

"What about the knife?" I asked.

Granny rubbed her chin. "I once saw an episode of *Murder She Wrote* where the murderer thought they killed the victim until he jumped up."

"So maybe then she swung the anchor at him," Aurora said.

"These are all good motives. But how'd Kathy get the knife?" I asked.

"She had to be at the picnic," Aurora said. "When she saw Jerry, maybe then she went and got the strawberry pie knife and lured him into the mangroves."

"Okay, anything else?" I was tired and needed to collapse on my couch with my pets.

"That boat is key," Aurora said, watching me suppress a yawn.

"Sounds like I need to visit the marina to see if any boats have been rented lately."

"Do you need a disguise?" Aurora asked.

"No disguise," I said. "Just going to be my plain self and see where that takes me."

Henrietta covered her mouth. Granny managed to keep silent. Aurora cleared her throat.

"Okay. That may not work. Any other ideas?"

"I know Brad leaves the side door unlocked occasionally," Granny said. "We can sneak in tomorrow, get to the files, and see who rented boats lately."

"I'm not going to ask how you know about the marina's side door," I said. "I can bring a glass cutter, just in case the door is locked. With all the boats gone missing, the broken window won't draw much attention, especially if none of the boats are gone."

"I'll let you all be my backup. I'll take the dinghy out around midnight," I said. "I'll park at the west side of the marina and try the side door backing up to the Grand Canal. I'm afraid Amos McNulty may be sleeping nearby in his cruiser."

"Old man McNulty? He has to be pushing a hundred by now," Granny said.

"At least he'll be snoring before midnight," Aurora said.

"And age has nothing to do with him napping on night watch," Granny said. "That man seemed to be born sleeping. He made a great beat cop, but he's not a detective, and he knows it. He falls asleep the minute he unfastens his seatbelt and sleeps through most of his stakeouts."

I stood up straight and looked at the three ladies. "Then it's settled. Tomorrow it is."

I heard Granny's chair scrape the wood floor as she stood. A glint of excitement lightened her eyes as she reached for my hand and squeezed it.

"Be careful."

I nodded.

Aurora reached into her large fake Michael Kors bag and pulled out a walkie-talkie.

She slid it across the table toward me.

"Is that a walkie-talkie?"

"Yes."

"Where in the world—"

Granny grabbed it. "Aw! Your granddad bought it for you years ago when we took you to Disney World. You were too young for a cell phone."

"And my dad bought them at Granny's garage sale," Aurora added.

"You know I'm old enough for a cell phone now?" I looked back at Aurora and Granny.

"Sure, we can text. But I thought about a backup plan in case your cell runs out of juice."

Aurora was referring to the constant drain of my cell phone battery. Most of the time, the phone was powered off because I forgot to charge it.

To prove her point, Aurora walked over to the front door and retrieved my backpack from the hook. She reached in the side pocket and removed my iPhone, then held it up. "See, it's off. No power. I tried texting you before we came over. You never replied. So I texted Granny."

Granny reached in her silk blouse and pulled out her mobile phone.

"Unless you have a pocket in your bra or a holster, I don't want to know where you keep that device," Henrietta said.

Granny read her text and laughed.

I shrugged. "Point made." I snatched the small black walkie-talkie and turned it on. I heard a buzzing sound and feedback, but I also heard background noise. It sounded like a boat motor.

"Where's the other one?"

"Oops, I must have left it in my canoe."

"You rowed over here?" I walked over to my window, my two pets trailing me. When I pulled back the curtain, I saw her lime green canoe resting on the beach.

"I needed the exercise." Aurora joined me at the window.

I heard crackling sounds from the walkie-talkie. I turned to Aurora. "You left it on?"

"I may have. I was testing them."

We both turned back to the window.

I saw the source of the motor sound. A boat had moored close to Aurora's canoe.

When the motor's sound subsided, I squinted and saw four shadows bobbing on the boat.

"Who's that?" Aurora asked, leaning in close to the windowpane.

The bright sunlight shone on the boaters' backs, creating silhouettes. But I knew that boat and that figure. My heart sank. "Deputy Drew, and it looks like a female and two smaller passengers," I said, craning my neck to see through the palm fronds.

As I looked closer, I realized the two smaller figures were the backs of the chair cushions.

"Shhh," Granny said, pointing to the walkie-talkie, as she walked up behind me.

"See you later tonight," Drew's familiar voice crackled across the talkie.

When I turned up the volume on the device, I realized the group of women in my kitchen had stopped talking and were watching me. My face flamed.

Who was Drew talking to?

I stared at the walkie-talkie. There were scuffling noises radiating through the talkie, and when I checked the window, I'm pretty sure I saw the woman lean in and kiss Drew on the check.

A kiss?!

"Yes, dear," a soft, unfamiliar female voice replied, "tonight."

All I could do was gape my mouth open as my world spun out of control.

CHAPTER THIRTEEN

"Mo, are you okay?" Aurora placed her hand on my shoulder. "Do you want to sit down?

I twisted my body away from her touch. All of a sudden, my apartment felt tiny. The walls were closing in. And it was so stuffy I couldn't breathe. My throat had a huge lump in it, and I fought hard not to let the tears well in my eyes.

But all I could think about were Dana's words: *He was with a tall girl in boots. He didn't wave. She wore boots....* And now there was a mystery woman outside my apartment on the Bay in Drew's boat with him. *And she's tall, and she's wearing boots!*

I reached for the corner of my chintz chair, swung around, and sat in it. I felt as if I had been punched in the stomach and smacked in the face.

I'll see you tonight. Her four words which effectively rendered the last five months of my life null and void and probably ended my relationship with Drew. And she kissed him!

Three pairs of sympathetic eyes bore into me, as they gathered around the blue chintz chair.

"I'll get water." Henrietta turned toward the kitchen.

I shrank back into the cushions, blinked away tears, and

cleared my voice. I needed answers. "Well, this adds a new element to our investigation," I croaked.

Granny stepped back from me. "I'm going down there right now and talk to Deputy Drew Powell."

"No!" I leaped up and grabbed Granny's arm. Yeah, I panicked. In my mind, I saw Granny blindly approaching Drew and confronting the stranger.

"What's the plan then?" Granny asked. I could see the emotional pain in her periwinkle eyes and knew she must be feeling as awful as I was, seeing her granddaughter hurting. It was written all over her face.

I let go of her arm and walked over to the kitchen table. "I'll talk to Drew. None of you will. Promise?" My eyes focused on Aurora, then Granny.

They both nodded.

Granny ran her trembling fingers through her hair, transforming the short gray strands into a geriatric faux hawk.

That made me smile. I let out a deep breath.

Granny blinked and gave me a tight smile.

I grabbed the glass of water that Henrietta offered me and took a swig. "I'll need something stronger if we're going to add this new component to the equation."

"I'll drink to that," Granny said.

"Come on, Mo," Aurora said. "This isn't a piece of evidence or a clue to an investigation. This is Drew. I'm sure there's a logical explanation for this."

"Yeah, she's probably a new deputy," Granny said.

"I met the new deputy. He is a man. Deputy Cross." He had replaced retired Deputy Ted Walker.

"I understand. But you know Drew, and this is not what it seems," Aurora said.

I took a sip of the water. It was very odd behavior for Drew. And every bone, every nerve ending in my body was telling me that this was not a romantic interest, despite the woman's kiss goodbye. "She kissed him. What detective or co-worker kisses a partner goodbye?"

"She's got a point," Henrietta chimed in.

I thought about my relationship with Deputy Drew. It had moved beyond the kissing stage. Of course, when we did go to the next level, we were secretive about it. The few times Drew stayed at my apartment late, he parked his car in my neighbor's garage. I had a key to Mrs. Thompson's place, and she wasn't due back until July. So we often used her empty, uncluttered garage to keep our cars.

We had hidden our trysts. But really, what was the point? This was Bay Isles, and my café was 100 steps away from my apartment. Everything interesting in our village was a topic of conversation in my café.

At first, when Drew and I started dating openly, I had a few disapproving stares in my café. The residents of Bay Isles had some ancient ideas on relationships. Of course, over half the population had an AARP card, so that may have been a factor in our use of discretion.

"Well, there are many ways to interpret a kiss," Granny said.

I turned to her and waited.

"There's the *it-was-nice-working-with-you-tonight* kiss, and there's the *you're-a-star-witness* kiss, and *thanks-for-protecting-me* kiss.*" Granny's smile was not convincing.

"She's got a point," Aurora said. "If this is a new detective replacing Fancy Pants Lacey, then she may be leaning in for a thank-you kiss."

"Or if she's a suspect and Drew is schmoozing her, that may be part of his undercover act," Henrietta chimed in.

"I'm not sure of anything right now. I need to think." If anyone had told me it was possible to feel worse than I did right now, I would have to call him a liar. My insides ached. My throat was sore from not swallowing the lump piercing it.

"Okay. Let's leave Mo alone." Granny turned to grab her cane.

"Can someone check on the boat? Is Drew still out there? I can't bear to look out the window right now." I turned to Aurora.

"I'll check." Aurora walked over to the window facing the Bay and peeked out. "He's leaving now. Which would explain the motor noises we can hear in the walkie-talkie." Aurora pointed to the device now tossed on the blue chair.

"What about the girl?" Granny asked as she made her way to the window.

"She's walking toward the café. She must have parked there."

I jumped up and went to the window. A few minutes, later we saw the headlights of a black pickup truck leave the parking lot.

Aurora turned to me, her mouth dropped open. "Wasn't that Drew's truck she was driving?"

I nodded. My problems had just gotten a thousand times worse.

———

After the three left my apartment, with a new plan in place, I sank down in the kitchen chair and stared at my laptop. My brain was whirling so fast I was afraid it would spin out of my skull. Why was Drew's lady friend driving his pickup truck? And she was so friendly to him. He had called her sweetie, and he said he would see her later.

Kona, who was dozing at my feet, decided my lap was too

empty. He jumped onto it and nudged his head against my arm, almost jostling the mouse from my hand.

"What the hell was Drew doing?" I asked my cat. Kona purred.

"That's a fair question, isn't it?" One more good bump from Kona and my wireless mouse flew to the floor.

I dumped Kona off my lap and snatched the mouse.

"You little dickens," I scolded Kona as I picked him up and stroked his back.

I abandoned my work on the laptop and thought through the plan. We had all agreed to go forward with our next steps.

The next day, Aurora would visit Penny's house under the guise of delivering baked goods. Granny was going to get her nails done at the Island Salon, talk to Dana and summon up any new gossip about the dead reporter and Drew's mystery woman. Henrietta was cooking up a fantastic dinner for the next night that would melt Drew's heart.

And me, I had been researching on my laptop more about Jerry and the articles he had written. I was killing time until after midnight.

I had ditched the marina plan. I didn't feel like B&E, breaking and entering. Instead, I would sneak out in a few hours and take my stand-up paddleboard over to Fort DeSoto Park. It couldn't hurt to have a look around the area where the body was found. I'd take a fishing net and pole, my tickle stick and a flashlight. It's not uncommon to see fishermen using their SUP to catch lobsters at night.

After the group left, I had rigged my SUP board with a red milk carton crate attached to it. I used PVC tubes in the milk crate to help support my fishing pole and tickle stick, while the crate itself would store my supplies.

I actually planned to fish until I knew my cover was safe, so I had my fishing gear in the crate. I also had nighttime goggles and a stun gun (Granny's recommendation), a spotlight, night-time camera, a walkie-talkie, my cell phone, and a Yeti sack.

It didn't hurt to be prepared for unexpected creatures. I had also included in my crate a forty-eight-inch metal stick with a hooked end and snake tongs with a rubber-coated jaw. Just in case. Sharks didn't bother me; it was the snakes and gators I didn't want to catch me off guard.

The leather gloves were a gift from my Grandpa Lowe. They were lined with Kevlar and had extra-long cuffs to shield my wrists and forearms. Not only would a lobster not pinch me, but a snake would have trouble biting through the gloves. Also, if I found any evidence that the police missed, I wouldn't want my prints on it. With my waders on, I'd look like I was ready for war. I was protected and organized.

My water dog, Snickers, would accompany me. The crate with its lid would take up the back of the board and could double as a seat if I needed it. But I preferred to stand in the middle, and Snickers stood between me and the nose of the board. The platform had enough width for my loyal buddy and me and decent grip pads to assist with Snickers' balance.

As if Kona knew he would be left out of tonight's shenani-gans, he playfully batted his paw at my backpack. It tipped over, and my red moleskin notebook slipped out.

"You really need to go upstairs and play on your cat tree. You have a lot of energy tonight."

Kona slinked under my table, making Siamese noises, which meant he sounded like a whole alley full of cats.

"But since you've gotten my attention, let's review what we know so far," I said to my loyal audience of two, Snickers and Kona, both anxious to help.

I retrieved my red moleskin notebook. Under my list of names, I saw a note to call Christine. I looked at my watch: 9:15.

Would she still be up? I'd give it a shot.

She answered after the first ring. "Hello."

I placed my cell on speaker, so I could take notes. "Hi Christine, this is Molly. Is it too late to call?" Christine often filled in for the town's police dispatcher and worked part-time in the vet's office. She had access to files.

"No. I hate to admit it, but I was binge-watching a series on Netflix."

"Anything good?"

"My latest addiction is *Orange is the New Black*. I've watched three hours straight, and I have to get up early. But it's as good as they say. Have you seen it?"

"No, not yet. It's on my list." But even as I said the words, I wondered when my life would ever settle down enough to watch TV.

"Well, I won't take long, so you can get back to Litchfield Penitentiary." I smiled. At least I knew the setting of the series.

"What's up? Are you calling about the reporter?"

"Yes, did you get the autopsy results yet?" I had asked her earlier if she had access to read through the notes.

"We have a temporary medical examiner during the Easter break, and he's swamped right now until Rick is back on Monday. But there were some preliminary findings."

Rick Dodgson, known as Dr. D, was the county's regular ME. We lived in a small county, and our medical examiner was also the local vet. He had moved to Bay Isles from the Northwest, something we had in common. However, Dr. D hadn't seemed to get acclimated to Florida like I had. He still wore cashmere sweaters with cuff-bottom wool trousers.

"Since Dr. D is away for the Easter holiday, has the state ME helped out?"

"Deputy Lucky has asked for their assistance. You should ask him."

"You know how he hates my meddling." I laughed.

"And he should." Christine's tone was rueful.

"But you and I are family." I have five aunts, and my dad's oldest sister, Sherry, had married Christine's uncle. They're divorced, but Christine and I always joked that we were step-cousins, even if it was for only two years.

"That we are."

"Can you tell me if there was any trace evidence?" Before I went snooping tonight, I wanted to know what they had recovered from the scene.

"There were several things. But I really haven't been able to get a good look at the file. As you know, Penny's fingerprints were on the knife, and there were others."

"Any that have been identified?"

"I can't say yet. Maybe just a few of the ladies in the park that day."

I nodded and then answered, "Yes, of course. What about his blood samples? Anything in it? Barbiturates? Narcotics? Were there any skin or saliva samples? And the soil on his shoes? Or anything under his fingernails?" I knew that any trace of soil could determine information about where it came from, like from the beach or from a barn.

"The toxicology reports aren't back yet. But his fingers were stained with tobacco. A smoker. Nothing unusual on the shoes. Sandspurs, the things you expect from walking around the park near the saltwater."

"Any bruising?" The fatal injuries may not have been the only evidence found on Jerry's body. I knew from my conversations with my Aunt Tammera if there had been a fight or physical struggle, patterns of bruising could give an indication of what happened.

"Just the one under his eye and on his knee. But you already should know about those."

Good thing Christine couldn't see me, because my face had flushed bright red.

"He grabbed my costume tail. What was I to do?"

"I hear ya. I'd have done the same thing. Too bad it was only an Easter basket you clobbered him with."

Ouch. Did everyone in Bay Isles know about my confrontation with the victim? That gave me a thought. If he bothered me enough to smack him over the head with a basket, who else had he harassed? "Do you know why Drew mentioned he was hit with a heavy object? Was that what killed him? Since he also had a knife wound?"

"I did overhear Rick — I mean Dr. D — talking to Deputy Cross. He mentioned something about an artifact. I assumed the Civil War reenactment was stocked, but I don't think they leave the guns and swords lying around."

"I didn't see anything near the body. Did they find the second weapon and were there fingerprints on it?"

"No and no. They didn't find the weapon that caused the blow. Seems if the knife laceration didn't kill him, the final blow did."

"Are they sure Mary Dedham's strawberry pie knife was one of the weapons?"

"Yes. Dr. D is also a certified pathologist, and he verified the serrated blade tip fit the wound."

We were silent for a few minutes.

"Was there anything else?"

"Oh, one more thing: They found pink fibers under his fingernail."

"Hmmm. Thanks, Christine. I owe you. Let's have coffee at the café one day and catch up."

"Ok, sounds good. I'll see you at your anniversary party. I wouldn't miss it."

"See you then. Goodbye."

"Good night."

I clicked off my cell phone and walked into the kitchen. If I was to paddle over to Fort De Soto Park and still manage to fight off the mosquitoes and no-see-ums, I needed to have something in my stomach.

As I stared into my near-empty refrigerator, I thought about Christine's last comment. Pink fibers.

Pink was the favorite spring color of the Bay Isles women and little girls. Even Lucy's two daughters wore matching pink jumpers. Come to think of it, wasn't Penny wearing pink designer jeans too? With a wine-colored top? Yes. I recalled that the Ralph Lauren pants had fit Penny's waist perfectly but were too tight over her behind, the pink fibers threatening mutiny.

Kathy Waves had been dressed in a long Pepto-Bismol pink flowing skirt with a rhinestone-studded matching tank top.

I bent over and petted Snickers and whispered in his ear, "Just between you and me, I think these two ladies are related somehow."

CHAPTER FOURTEEN

Ten minutes before midnight, I carried my paddleboard to the bay and pushed off. I glanced sideways as I paddled. At this late hour on a Sunday night, Main Street was deserted, all the shop windows dark.

Nature was cooperating. The night was moonless, and left-over clouds from the afternoon's storms obstructed the natural glow from the water's reflections.

Thank goodness I had strong standup paddling skills. I could easily maintain good board balance while fishing. Whenever I went out, I tried hard not to find myself in water conditions that were above my skill level. I was one of the best SUP boarders around, but a capsized board would dump my gear in my crate into the water, and it could be difficult to flip back over with my fishing poles attached.

"Good job, Snicks," I whispered to my partner in crime.

Snickers had always been a water dog. I took him to the beach daily. He had gotten on his first paddleboard when he was just a tiny pup. My encouraging words of love and patience helped Snickers become a styling SUP pup, and now as an adult dog, he stood sturdy and confident, staring out into the water with an eye on the lookout.

I moved my paddle efficiently through the small surf, slapping the ubiquitous mosquitoes that occasionally nipped my face where my only exposed skin provided plenty of dining opportunities.

Twenty minutes later, as I approached the park, I scanned the bank from my vantage point on the high board, my flashlight trained on the shore to reflect the telltale glint of gator eyes. The last thing I needed was a hungry alligator on my hands.

As I swung the beam back and forth across the beach, I didn't see anything move. No noise, not even a night bird tweeting.

Drawing near to shore, I caught the scent of the swampy algae that often formed on the north beach at certain times. It smelled like mold and dirty socks.

Fort DeSoto Park was wrapped in three miles of beautiful white-sand beaches, and the park was made up of five islands totaling over a thousand acres, anchored by the main island, Mullet Key, where the park's namesake fort and main beaches were located.

I had approached the park from the north, which felt a little eerie at this hour. Camping was allowed on the island, so I wasn't trespassing. I paddled toward the less-crowded East Beach on the bayside, which was more convenient for me to check out the picnic area but not easily accessible while camping in the park's campground. That left me alone to explore the area where Jerry's body was found.

The wind was whipping up high waves as I approached the shore, making the water choppy. Usually, the paddleboard entrance to the beach provides a breathtaking experience. No matter how many times I visited the park, it always had the "wow" effect on me, even at night. But tonight something was different.

I jumped off the paddleboard, out of breath, and a moment later, Snickers was at my side. The beach was narrow during high tide.

I secured the paddleboard to the shore and whispered to Snickers, "Let's go."

My handheld flashlight beam was strong enough to search the mangroves in front of me. After several attempts at different paths that went nowhere, I found the way to the picnic area. A small headlight, which I chose not to turn on yet, was strapped around my baseball cap. We continued with caution along the path, my eyes taking in every footprint and looking for any clues.

A movement behind the mangroves caught my eye, and Snickers started to growl. I held out the flashlight and pointed the beam on the path toward the picnic tables. I inched forward.

"Shhh," I whispered to Snickers. I removed one of my gloves and tucked it in my waders.

I was so focused on the shadow I imagined behind the bushes that I momentarily lost my balance. I teetered in the sandy soil, but once I regained my footing, I took a step and caught my foot on a tree root.

My face hit the soft ground, and the flashlight rolled from my hand.

"Damn."

I crawled to the flashlight, while Snickers slammed into me. I immediately swept the beam and saw no one or nothing. I scrambled to my feet, stumbling a few feet forward when the pain in my wrist hit me. I twisted my left hand and winced at the aches in my joints.

"Ouch. I think I bruised my wrist," I whispered.

I removed my other glove and ran my hand along my

injured wrist, and fine grains of sand that had adhered to it flecked off. "What's this?" I whispered.

A large piece of shell stuck to my palm sparkled in the light, and at first, I wasn't sure what I was looking at. I slipped the nugget into my pants pocket and zipped it up.

I searched the sand for any other unusual items. The path looked well-traveled, so identifying different types of shoe prints would be futile. Besides, the deputies would have taken shoe impressions, and Christine would share the findings over a latte.

I wasn't sure what I was looking for, but I knew the small treasure in my pocket was important. My hand had accidentally been pushed into the sand deep enough to recover this tiny gem of possible evidence.

After searching the picnic area for a good twenty minutes, I came up with nothing else.

I was heating up in my protective gear and I needed to get home and ice my wrist. I reached under my waders and pulled on my pants, unsticking them from my sweaty thighs.

As we left the area, Snickers chased a small rodent into the bushes.

"Come Snickers," I said softly.

I used the flashlight beam to check out the scrubby bushes. I assumed he had chased a bunny, similar to Penny's story about her dog Gucci, but I had yet to see a rabbit on the island. A lot was going through my mind as I carefully crept forward to find Snickers.

"There you are. Do I need to put a leash on you? Good boy," I said. As I bent down to pet him, his head snapped up and smacked me under the chin. Ouch, he had a hard skull!

Before I realized what was happening, Snickers shot across the opening, a brown blur in the night, and stopped behind a clump of mangroves.

When I reached him, I was out of breath and my wrist was throbbing. I was about to scold Snickers and tell him that his behavior had been wrong when I noticed what he was doing.

He was digging in the soft, sandy soil around the picnic table. I gave him a wide berth, as he always came up with exciting items when his nose found something.

When Snickers' paws quit digging, I leaned over, and my light caught something long and skinny in his mouth. At first, I thought he had uncovered a giant worm, but on further inspection, it was a string.

"What do you have there?" I knelt beside the small hole.

Snickers wagged his tail.

The string was attached to something the size of a football. When I brushed the sand and dirt away, I realized what I was holding.

A tennis shoe. The string turned out to be a shoelace. It was attached to a white sneaker.

I closed my eyes to think. Who had worn tennis shoes to the festival?

Everyone.

"Does this have anything to do with the murder, Snickers?" In any case, touching a shoe belonging to a possible murderer rated high on my "ick" factor.

Who would want to hold a shoe worn by a stranger, especially a possible murderer? With my gloved hand, I pulled a plastic grocery bag from my pocket and carefully placed the shoe in it.

My heart was beating fast. The shoe was probably nothing. But what if it did belong to a suspect? Had the detectives and officers missed it? Had the murderer buried it? But why?

I put my face up to Snickers and stared him in his big brown eyes to get his attention. "You did good."

He stared back at me for several seconds, not blinking or

looking away, then wagged his tail. I kissed his forehead. "Let's go, partner."

Before we made it back to the SUP, I had decided to call Drew. But then how would I explain why I was at the park at this hour?

I knew it was right to take the shoe, which could be possible evidence, with me. I would call Drew and explain I had been at the park with Snickers, and he dug it up.

Snickers let out a soft whine. When I looked at him, he wagged his tail before nudging me toward the SUP and letting out a soft bark. *Woof!*

"Are you ready to go?"

His lips pulled back in a silent snarl as his eyes stared out toward the water.

I turned my attention in that direction, and thirty feet to the left of my beached SUP was a small fishing vessel. It was moving toward us.

"Down," I whispered.

Snickers dropped his belly to the ground, and I followed. I glanced over at the boat, and its sole occupant had apparently anchored.

A man who appeared to be tall from my crouching position came on to the shore.

I noticed the lack of fishing gear in his empty hands.

When he turned in our direction, I sat up and told Snickers to greet.

Snickers stood up and put his nose to the air, his head turning toward the approaching man.

"Hold it right there," he yelled at Snickers as he threw his arms out in front of him, his fingers fanned open.

As Snickers cautiously approached, the man kicked at him. Snickers snarled, but I yanked him back in time, before he could bite the guy.

I grabbed my taser gun from my pocket. "You kick at my dog again," I hissed, "and I'll fry you like a mosquito stuck in a bug zapper."

With my other hand, I turned on my headlamp to show the taser gun pointed at him.

An angry but familiar voice startled me. "So this is what you locals do for fun at night?"

It was Tommy Pierson.

CHAPTER FIFTEEN

I slipped the taser gun into my pocket. "Snickers and I were night shelling." I was on the defensive before I could stop myself.

"So you say."

Angry at being caught in the park at night for no apparent reason, I retorted, "What are *you* doing here?"

"I was restless." Tom bent down and rubbed Snickers behind his ear. "I haven't been sleeping well. I've been worried about the contest. I took the boat out to check out the park for the event and to do some night fishing."

"Where's Kathy?" I snapped, still uncertain why Tommy would be at the park alone at this hour.

"She's um—" he looked down as he kicked at the sand with his bare feet. "She drinks a lot. She's been asleep since seven."

"I see." My uneasiness subsided a bit. I resisted the urge to challenge him on his relationship with Kathy. But right now, I needed to get out of the mosquito-infested beach. "Do you want to grab coffee? I have the keys to my café, and I make a pretty darn good latte, and besides, I'm not sure I want to paddle back to my place. We could put the SUP inside your boat and be at my café in ten minutes." My bruised wrist could use a break.

Tom's phone buzzed in his pocket, and he had it out in a flash, tapping away and ignoring me for a second.

"Sorry," he said. "The manager at the hotel said he heard loud music from our room. She must be awake."

"Right…" I said, drawing the word out.

"I can still drop you and Snickers off at your beach."

"Deal. Let's get going and away from these giant bat-mosquitos."

"Let me help you with the board," he said, as we each grabbed an end of the SUP. "You must be great at paddle-boarding if you can fish on this thing." He pointed at the crate.

"I can hold my own." I shone the light on the beach in front of us to light the way.

Beyond the sea oats, out of sight, someone fired a shot.

Tommy's head jerked up, eyes instantly alert.

I felt a jittery feeling in my chest, as if a sharp-clawed animal was scratching my breastbone.

"What the hell?" Tommy said, pointing his flashlight toward the brush.

"Someone's most likely hunting gators. The visitors to the area don't know any better. Or it could be poachers."

"With a man murdered in the park yesterday, you seem awfully calm."

This caused a chill to run up my spine. It wasn't so much his words as the way he said it. I suddenly felt vulnerable. I hadn't seen or spoken with Tommy Pierson in almost three years. But deep down, I knew he meant well, despite him falling for the likes of Kathy.

He was quick to pick up the thought behind his words. "I mean here we are in the park at night, and we clearly heard what could have been a gunshot, or maybe it was a firecracker."

No matter how intrigued I was by finding Tommy Pierson out at night without Kathy, there was still something about his late-night presence that unsettled me. "We hear shots every now and then, and it usually turns out to be nothing more than a local chasing a gator or a coyote off their property."

Tommy's tone simmered down. "So you really have gators here with the saltwater?" he asked, nervously looking around.

"Yes. There are enough small retention ponds and fresh-water canals and channels around to have started a small population of gators. There aren't as many in the park as you think, but occasionally a camper will spot one."

"And that's what you think—" he nodded his shoulder toward the gunshot sound we'd heard moments before "—they're shooting at?"

"Most likely. Or possibly a camper scaring off a coyote."

"Are there alligator poachers here?"

"Occasionally we get poachers who want the meat, or they think they can skin a gator in hopes of it being used for a new line of designer handbags or worse," I said and shuddered, "cowboy boots."

Tommy laughed. "Maybe I should check it out. Kathy would die for a new gator bag."

I smiled, and for the first time, I realized Tommy was wearing black dress slacks and a light blue short-sleeved polo shirt. Classic and preppy, but not fishing gear.

"You weren't planning on fishing, were you?"

He glanced down at his pants. "No. And if you allow me to take you and Snickers back to your café, you'll see that I don't even have poles in my boat, but I can explain."

I nodded. "Let's go before the poachers or campers make their way over here."

Once Snickers, my SUP, and I were settled on the boat, Tommy motored slowly away from Fort DeSoto Park. The grocery bag with the tennis shoe was tucked safely in my Yeti dry sack.

Tommy eased the tiny boat onto the open water and slowly picked up speed until my ginger-colored braid whipped behind me like a striking snake.

"Where'd you get the boat?" I asked over the dull roar of the motor.

"I rented it all week. I thought it would make me feel like a local, motoring around by boat."

"Does it?"

He pushed the throttle forward and increased the speed. "Sometimes."

"If you really want to be like a local, you'll need a golf cart and a cane."

He smiled. "There are a lot of retirees here, aren't there?"

Before I could answer, we turned the corner toward the south side of Bay Isles, where several channels connect, and where it became a slow wake zone.

As he slowed the boat, we saw a small airboat peeking out of one of the canals.

We were about twenty feet from the shore, and I checked the mangroves lining the bank. I didn't spot a campsite.

I whispered to Tommy. "This is an area of freshwater pools on one of the islets, and where we often see gators. Let's get closer to them."

"You want to turn into the channel?"

"Sure. Let's see who it is."

Tommy turned and slowed his boat, and as the two men in a boat came into view, I had to wonder if they were poachers. They weren't locals that I recognized, but I waved.

When the men saw us approach, they didn't wave back.

"You sure this is a good idea?" Tommy asked. "It's dark. They don't know who we are."

"If they shot a gator, we would see it in their boat."

"And why would you want to know that?"

"Well, for starters, it's against the law."

"What are you, a private investigator now?"

I didn't answer.

"Oh, that's right, Kathy mentioned you are dating that cop."

"Shhh." We were getting close enough to the boat that the men could hear us.

"You two lost?" the skinnier of the two men said.

When we got close enough to shine a light on the boat, I could see that both men looked fiftyish with baseball caps over silver hair. The one speaking probably topped out over six feet, but it was hard to tell since both men were sitting down.

"We were going to ask you the same thing," I said and looked over at Tom and winked.

"Nah. We ain't lost. We just fishing," the bigger guy replied.

I nodded.

"You didn't hear a gunshot, did you?" Tommy asked.

"Who's asking?" The skinniest one sat up taller.

"I'm Tom, and this is, um, Mo." Tommy hesitated and reached over to Snickers. "And this is our co-captain."

Snickers didn't wag his tail and stood tall.

When the men didn't reply with their names, I opened my mouth and started yakking. "We were just taking a midnight cruise. We were planning on paddleboarding," I said, pointing to the board. "Something I've always wanted to do. Being out on the water at night, under the stars, is so peaceful and romantic." I hoped they were buying it.

"What can I say? We were looking for the perfect spot," Tommy said, shrugging.

I gave him points for managing to follow along with my fib.

The taller man moved, and I caught sight of a tarp behind them. Despite the dim light, I was able to take in the image without any trouble. As my eyes probed deeper behind him, the man started to puff up and stared directly at me. His eyes widened a little, and I could tell that he figured out that I knew what they were doing. He licked his lips and glanced at his pal.

"Well, you two get on your way," the skinny one said.

"I didn't catch your names," I said.

"We ain't thrown them out. Now be careful backing out of here. These canals can be dangerous."

"Look—" I said, but Tommy held up his arm, signaling me to shut up.

"See ya," Tommy said.

The big guy mumbled something as he wiggled a finger at me, as we pulled away.

"Did he just say, 'Snitches end up in ditches'?" I whispered to Tommy when we were clear of the other boat.

"It sounded that way to me."

CHAPTER SIXTEEN

Tommy and I rode the remainder of the short boat ride to the beach behind my apartment in silence.

I had a ton of questions; the least of them, now not so important, was why was Tommy at the park tonight? And before I left the boat, I needed to find out.

"Over there is a good spot," I pointed to the open beach in the bay behind my complex.

"I still can't get over all the little bays and inlets around here," Tommy said. "I had no idea."

"That's why it's called Bay Isles. I live on the island on the bay side. Even though water flows from the Gulf to fill the inlets and bays, we don't get the higher waves."

"So no surfing?"

"No surfing." I pointed to shore as the boat came closer. "I love it during low tide; I can walk in. And the beach is so expansive, you could land a plane on it."

Tommy killed the engine, and I hopped in the water to help maneuver the boat closer to shore. He handed me the anchor, and I secured it.

"Aren't you afraid of stepping on a stingray? Or worse, a shark?" Tommy asked.

"I do see them out here occasionally, but the water is a bit cool right now. It's probably still in the 70s. Plus, I shuffle my feet through the sand, so I don't surprise a stingray. I've been stung before, and the sharp barbs on their stingers are painful."

"Didn't that Crocodile Hunter guy die from a stingray barb?"

"Yes. Steve Irwin. But he was holding it against his chest at the time. I don't plan on holding a wild stingray."

"Alligators, stingrays, sharks, mosquitos the size of bats, lizards everywhere… I'm telling you, Molly, you're living in a tropical zoo. Your dad would be proud of you."

The comment about my dad took me momentarily aback. "Why my dad?"

"Didn't you tell me that he always said he preferred your adventurous side over a girlie-type daughter?"

I felt a blush creep up my neck, and I was thankful for the dimly lit beach.

While we removed the paddleboard, Snickers made his way to the nearest seagrass.

"Even under that hat and in the dark, I can see how much you remind me of your dad."

I tilted my head as I grabbed the paddleboard.

"Don't get me wrong; you have your dad's work ethic and your mom's good looks."

I shrugged and blushed more but stayed silent.

Tommy studied me for a moment. "You really don't get it. You've always been the most confident and hottest girl in the place. And I'm glad you have that deputy guy."

"Drew," I mumbled.

"Right. You really deserve a great guy. And for the record,

your dad would be proud of you owning your own café. I know I am."

It was the second time in a day someone had commented about my dad and how he would be proud of me. Back in Oregon, I focused on my college work, and I rarely had time to think about my dad. Now it seemed as if he was on my mind a lot. My new local friends and now my past friends had found a way to make me take a hard look at my dad's past.

"Hello Mo. Earth to Molly." Tommy waved his hand in front of me.

"I'm sorry. I'm just tired. It's been a long day."

Tommy nodded and leaned over my paddleboard lying on in the sand. "What's this?" Tommy pointed to one of Snickers' retractable dog leashes. Attached to the end of the strap was an old, orange vinyl-covered barbell. The ends of the red leash were frazzled. But it worked fine.

"It's what you think it is." I smiled.

He scrunched up his eyes. "Is that a do-it-yourself paddle-board anchor?"

"Yup. Not too shabby for a couple of bucks and a few minutes of my time." I thought about the muddy and sandy bottom around the park and knew a lightweight fluke anchor was the best option for that area if you moored a boat there. My thought on an anchor being used as a weapon to hit Jerry's head was still an active one.

"You never cease to amaze me. I knew you were always creative."

"You sure you don't want that latte or a pastry?" I had a lot of questions for Tommy.

"I'll take a raincheck."

"Will Kathy be upset that you were out?" I didn't want Tommy to leave before he answered a few questions.

"She probably fell back asleep or went to a beach bar."

"Looking for you?"

"No, looking for a drink," he said sadly.

I frowned. "Hey, I know it's none of my business, but are you two okay?"

He shrugged. "Just pre-wedding jitters, and well, my business isn't going well."

I nodded and bit my lower lip. "You said you'd explain why you were out boating tonight."

"Next question."

"Seriously. We used to be so close. I would have taken your word that you were fishing."

"Even without poles?"

"Well…" I kicked at the sand. "That does need explaining."

He turned and looked directly into my eyes. "Why would you have taken my word? We ended poorly. I'm so sorry. I was a fool that last year of college. I wouldn't blame you if you never forgave me."

"Hey, it was over between you and me. As we once said, we were not going to be together." My hands felt clammy.

He nodded his head. "We did care for each other once," he said, much to my surprise. "You know, if you take away the fact that I was a total cheat and an occasional liar, I'm actually a good man."

"And conceited," I laughed, then asked, "So clear up one lie, what were you really looking for tonight?"

Tommy searched the horizon, and then his eyes met mine again. "Truth be told, I was worried about the event this week because of the boat thieves."

"What do the stolen boats have to do with it?"

"Mo, don't you see? This is a boating event too. Participants and spectators could be worried enough not to bring their boats in with all that's going on. Half a dozen boats have gone missing, and now there's a dead guy. Not the perfect news you want before one of our biggest events. When I said my business wasn't going well, I wasn't putting it lightly. A low attendance could bankrupt us and put me out of business this weekend."

I had a good idea what Tommy was going through. I had seen local businesses collapse over an extended Red Tide or hurricane season where the tourists and conventioneers canceled their trips to the Bay Isles area. "I understand. But that doesn't explain why you were out by the park. Wouldn't you be holding a watch by the marinas?"

"I've been going out at night to see if I can catch anyone or see anything."

"So now you're the vigilante?"

"If that's what it takes to prevent additional bad press."

"So why stakeout at the park?"

He looked uncomfortable, like I hit a sore spot.

"I was following you." He smacked at a mosquito on his forehead. His expression was gloomy.

I felt the color rush into my cheeks. "What? Why?" Inside my mind, I heard a string of profanities, but I kept that to myself. I looked at Tommy, my mouth agape.

He shook his head.

I couldn't look in his eyes. Instead, I turned and glanced around the beach and saw Snickers lying by the footpath to the boardwalk. When he saw me look at him, he stood up and came over and stood by my side.

"Well?" I said, turning back to Tommy.

A mosaic of light and shadows danced around Tommy from the water's reflection, but when he spoke, his eyes were clear and moist. "It's the truth that I can't sleep at night, and I'm restless. That led me to rent this boat and keep a lookout for the boat thieves. I've been out a few nights in a row now. And it's been quiet and boring. Until tonight. I saw you paddleboarding. You were so concentrated on your efforts that you didn't see me when I came out of Little McPherson's Bay."

I bent over slightly and put a tentative hand on Snickers' back and stroked. Snickers looked up at me, unblinking, then turned his attention to Tommy. I made no comment.

Tommy continued. "I stayed back a good distance and let you have space. After twenty minutes or so, I saw that you were headed to the picnic area on the north side of the Fort De Soto Park. And I had to wonder why *you* were out at night sneaking around on your SUP board. I was intrigued and curious. You were smart to bring your fishing poles as a cover, but you never once dropped a line in the water, even when you paddled through a school of snook."

I stared at Tommy, my eyebrows raised.

"So I know you don't owe me an explanation, but I have to ask you again the same question — what were you and Snickers looking for?"

"All I can say is the same thing you were looking for." I felt guilty knowing there was a tennis shoe in my Yeti duffle bag that Snickers uncovered. But I planned to take it tomorrow morning to Drew at the police station. Or better yet, I would invite Deputy Drew over for breakfast and give it to him after I snapped a few photos of it. Plus, I wanted to talk to Drew about the woman he had been with.

"Touché," Tommy said. His cell phone chimed, and he looked at it and said, "Kathy."

"Go," I said, then I had a thought. "Wait. Do you know if Kathy wears white tennis shoes?"

"Yes, I suppose so. Why?"

I shrugged. "It's nothing. But can you check to see if any are missing?"

He cocked his head. "Sure."

"Thanks for the lift. You better get going; you have some explaining to do to Kathy," I said and leaned in for a quick hug.

Tommy whispered in my ear, "You're going to have some explaining to do yourself." He lifted his head, and his eyes went behind me.

I turned around and saw the silhouette of Deputy "Lucky" Drew Powell standing at the edge of the path leading to the boardwalk.

Snickers made a beeline toward Drew, wagging his tail. And I trailed behind him, the Yeti duffle bag left in the red crate temporarily forgotten.

CHAPTER SEVENTEEN

"Hey," I said, in the hushed silence that surrounded us.
He didn't reply.

"This is a surprise. What are you doing here?" I said nervously.

"I could be asking you the same thing. But first, who was that?" He pointed toward the shore and Tommy's boat in the distance. "Was that your ex?"

"Who? Tommy? Um, yes. Funny story. I was out fishing with Snickers, and then I saw a boat, and it was Tommy. And he was fishing too."

Drew looked at me silently, puzzled.

Feeling self-conscious, I ran a hand through my newly-cut, short, frizzy hair.

"Oh, and there's a possible problem you may have."

"Now what?"

"There's a fishing boat moored in the inlet outside the north side of the park, and I think they have a gator or something in their boat."

"And you know this how?"

I nodded toward my SUP beached behind us.

He looked at me but didn't reply.

"Drew, I know this is a complicated story. Coffee?" I gestured toward the path to the café.

He shook his head.

He was starting to annoy me. "Are you going to say anything?" I whispered.

"It's late. Let me walk you to your apartment," he said in a hoarse voice, sounding exhausted.

We started up the path to my place, Snickers running up ahead.

When we got inside the front door, I saw that Drew's exhausted voice matched his appearance. His uniform was crumpled, and I could only assume he hadn't slept in days.

"Molly, I care about you. And I'm not stalking you, I promise. I drove by and saw the light on in your kitchen, so I stopped. When I knocked, you didn't answer, and Snickers didn't bark. That's when I heard voices out back." His pleasant voice was low in my ear.

"I didn't say I thought you were stalking me." But I wondered if Tommy had been. "I get it. You're a cop. You're out all night, keeping everyone safe." And there's the mess of a murder to solve and boat thieves to find.

"I'm too tired to ask you about your so-called fishing adventure. Can we talk tomorrow?"

I didn't like the defeat I saw in his eyes. Or was he just tired? I couldn't let him go without asking a few questions of my own. I knew I'd never sleep if I didn't ask.

There was no way around the burning question I had, so I got right to the point.

"Earlier tonight, I saw you on your boat moored behind my apartment, and you weren't alone."

"What exactly are you asking?" There was a hint of an amused smile forming on his lips.

"Well…this is personal, Drew, but —" I struggled to complete a sentence, and my voice actually sounded steady despite the fist that would not stop squeezing my stomach.

"—the answer to 'was that a date' is no," he said.

I was glad to hear it, but I shrugged to convey the pretense that it didn't matter. But it did.

"Do you have a new deputy?" I asked, picking a piece of grass off my shirt. So far, I hadn't seen anything in his eyes that made me think he had been on a date or that he was hiding something.

"Besides Deputy Cross?" he replied.

"Yes. I was wondering if the precinct had hired another deputy or detective. Perhaps a woman to replace Detective Lacey."

"No."

"Um, okay. Then I give up. Who was with you tonight? Or does our relationship not allow me to ask?"

He was staring at me, comprehension in his eyes. "You think Monica was a date?"

"It could be possible. We never talked about exclusivity. And who's Monica?"

He was looking at me as though he didn't know whether to laugh or be impressed. He wiped his hand across his mouth, a gesture I found extremely sexy.

"You know what I love about you, Mo? Your imagination and the way you can unravel evidence and make it almost stick."

I started to interrupt him, and he held up his hand. "Monica is not a date. It's complicated. It is business, but she's not a Bay Isles deputy." He stopped and smiled and shook his head.

My heart started beating again, and I exhaled.

He reached for my hand. He suddenly seemed a lot taller than his normal six-foot frame. He pulled me to him. "Despite your nosiness into my investigations and the severity of your hairstyle right now, you are the only one for me."

He ran his hand through my shorter hair. "You are disturbingly beautiful. I love your large green eyes and clear rosy skin. I love the smattering of freckles on the bridge of your nose. All twelve of them."

I gave a little cough, wondering where this was going, but I liked it.

"Mo, trust me, okay? I can't explain earlier tonight to you. It's complicated. Can you please stop snooping around? I worry about you," Drew said.

"Okay. I'll stay out of your business. I wouldn't want you losing any sleep over me."

"Believe me, if and when I ever find myself over you, the last thing I'll be thinking about is sleeping."

I squeezed his arm. He was so darn cute.

But what about the kiss? Didn't she give him a kiss on the cheek? What did that mean? How do I ask him about the kiss? "The way it looked. I thought—" I couldn't finish my sentence. "—I couldn't tell from the distance, but she seemed enamored with you." Enamored? That's all I could come up with?

A flicker of a smirk crossed Drew's dark face and died away. "Well, is that so? Again, this is a police matter, and when this investigation is complete, I'll explain. That's all I can say for now."

I felt my body relax a fraction. Police matters. Aurora had warned me that the *significant other* of a detective can feel they are traitorous. "It just seemed like more than police matters, that's all."

Drew looked quite amused now, off guard, trying to recall earlier in the night in his mind. Surely he would remember the goodbye kiss.

The light was back in Drew's face. "Oh yes," he agreed. "I

guess it may seem that way. But you have to trust me, Mo. I'm only trying to protect you and others." He sobered quickly. "What were you doing spying on me?"

"Well—" My lips curled in a mischievous smile.

"Don't answer that. I know you too well. And you have a way of getting your nose into everything. And some things are better just left unsaid."

I wanted desperately to know what was going on with the boat thieves and the murder investigation, so I asked, "How's it going? Any leads on possible suspects?"

"Do you mean are you a suspect in this case?" His eyes now lit up.

"No. You don't think I would have anything to do with this?"

Drew shook his head. "We ruled out you since you weren't at the park during the time the crime took place."

"So nice of you. Then why are deputies hanging around my café? I mean more than usual?" I had noticed there was always a sheriff's car parked outside the café.

"I assure you they're not watching you," he said.

"Uh-huh. That didn't seem convincing. Usually, our local police don't sit watch unless they suspect someone, or something is going on."

Drew shifted his feet. "When I came to the park yesterday, I hadn't seen you yet, but I saw your partner—"

"— Aurora," I said.

"Yes, Aurora. She ran off in the opposite direction when she saw Jerry. Like she was guilty or afraid."

"And this is your reason for suspecting Aurora?"

"I was searching through court records. I found a lawsuit where a dental firm is suing the newspaper for slander because it talked about how this dentist cheated his customers by using inferior products, but the suit named Jerry in particular. And guess who filed the suit?"

"I have no clue."

"It's your bakery partner's dad."

"Aurora's dad?" My mind was in a whirl. "That doesn't mean she knew the reporter." But even as I said the words, I knew that probably wasn't true.

"Look Mo, I love how you want to protect your friends and family, but I need you to sit tight for now. Can you please do that for me?"

I nodded.

"Can you promise me that you'll go to bed and stay there all night?"

"I know one way you can be sure of that," I murmured.

He raised his eyebrows. "Aren't you afraid that people would be talking about us if they see I stayed over all night? You know how this town can be."

I grinned. "I think that cat is already out of the bag." And secretly, for my sake, I hoped Dana would find out Drew had spent the night here.

"You don't care if people talk?"

"About me? After being a murder suspect last year and helping to solve crimes, I think that ship has already sailed."

He nodded. "I can't, Mo. I'm sorry. Not tonight."

I could feel my eyes moisten.

Drew sensed my sadness. He pulled me close to him like a magnetic charm and brushed his sweet lips against mine. I melted into his arms; my legs felt weak and my body drained.

Moments later, we stopped kissing.

He held me at arm's length, and I smiled.

"Goodnight, Mo." His voice was hoarse with arousal.

"Goodnight," I said, even though I really wasn't ready to say goodnight yet. "Drive safely. And see you at Granny's for dinner."

He leaned down and gave me a quick kiss.

Once he left, I went to the window. I stood there, watching him drive off in his patrol car.

I missed him already!

"I love you, Mr. Deputy 'Lucky' Drew Powell," I whispered once I saw his red taillights out of sight.

I paused. Then I realized I always asked about the murder case, even after getting caught sneaking out late at night with my ex-boyfriend.

CHAPTER EIGHTEEN

K ona gazed up at me with sleepy blue eyes. The brown and caramel cat was stretched out across the length of my thighs, and he had a look of utter contentment on his face. I shifted positions, and Kona hooked his paw over my leg as though to keep me from getting out of bed.

"Sorry, Kona. Time to wake up," I said as I threw back the sheet.

Kona bounded out of the bed, ready to start the day, or to be fed breakfast.

"I wish I had your energy," I mumbled.

Snickers barked, his tail swinging back and forth as he inched forward to kiss me.

"Okay. Give me a minute, and I'll let you out. I need to shower first."

I checked the clock and saw it was 7:30 a.m. I'd officially slept late.

"Dang, I overslept. But we were up past two. Weren't we?"

Snickers barked.

I took a quick, very hot shower and headed to the kitchen for a much-needed coffee. The entire time I was showering and dressing, I couldn't stop thinking about my conversation with Drew last night.

I felt a twinge of guilt for not telling Drew about the white sneaker. But I had other things on my mind, like his mystery woman. I planned to grab the Yeti duffle bag and take it to Drew.

After a quick cup of coffee and feeding my pets, I snagged a protein bar out of the cupboard. I unwrapped the snack and was munching on it as I approached my SUP moored onshore.

The board was still in the same position that I had secured it in over six hours earlier, but something looked different.

I stared at the empty board.

Everything was gone.

"Crap!" I said.

Snickers came to my side and cocked his head. "Someone took all my supplies. My fishing gear is gone. The crate is gone. And damn it, the Yeti dry bag is gone. The thief even stole your retractable leash," I said to my dog.

I bent over and picked up the orange weight. "But they left the barbell."

I scanned the beach, hoping to see the items dumped out along the shore, but no luck.

"Stupid. Stupid. Stupid." I shook my head and struggled to think about what I was going to tell Drew.

"Oh Lord, we've got to get cracking. Let's go to work."

Aurora and I were seated at the back of the coffee shop in a cozy corner table by the book nook. Bales came over and asked us what we wanted to drink. Aurora's cup of joe varied as much as her hair color these days.

"I'll take a triple venti lightly sweetened nonfat caramel macchiato, with room," Aurora said.

"Room for what?" I asked. "You have everything in that drink except the kitchen sink."

"She wants room to add more cream," Bales said. "You think Aurora has a weird java order, earlier today, I had a group of college kids from Florida State, and one gal asked for a triple long shot large, but in an extra-large cup, half caffeinated, double cupped, no sleeve, salted caramel, mocha latte with two pumps of white chocolate mocha for mocha and substitute two pumps of hazelnut for toffee nut, half whole milk and half breve with no whipped cream, extra hot, extra foam, extra caramel drizzle, extra salt, add a scoop of vanilla bean powder with light ice, well stirred. And oh, by the way, she had a free reward."

I heaved a sigh. "Hopefully, she didn't ask for a free refill." I smiled.

"Our free rewards have a lot of perks," Aurora said.

"Drink double espresso and do stupid things faster," Bales added.

I laughed and glanced out the window. A solo deputy car sat in the parking lot. For a moment, I thought about the shoe I had found at the park. I thought about Drew's conversation last night. I found myself wondering if Aurora had worn white tennis shoes to the festival. *Stop it!* I told myself. *Focus on helping her, if needed.*

My baristas were my best friends. I had planned to talk to Aurora about what Drew had mentioned last night.

"Mo, do you want to try our drink special today? After all Aurora and I came up with it in your honor," Bales said.

"What is it?"

"It's two shots espresso, pump of caramel, toasted marshmallow, and I top off the steamed milk to look like a bunny tail. It's called Fluffy Bunny Latte."

"Nice, I like it," I said.

"We thought you would," Aurora said.

I smiled. "What about the Cadbury Crème Egg Frappuccino? How's it selling?"

"Believe it or not, we have sold an inordinate amount," Bales said.

"I'll take the usual, thank you." My usual was a coffee with real cream, sweetener, and a smidgeon of cinnamon. I often thought about mixing it up and ordering my coffee another way. Especially after my coffee combination had become evidence in a murder a few months ago that put me on the suspect list.

I put the thought of the murder I had helped solve out of my mind and focused on my conversation with Aurora.

She was talking about her trip to Penny's house. I nodded. "So you went by Penny's house to deliver the cookies, and when you were unloading the pastry boxes in the kitchen, you overheard her in the living room talking to Lucy, right?"

"Yes. Penny got a call and went into the family room."

"So you overheard her talking to Lucy?"

"Yes, I heard her mention Lucy by name several times. I wanted to linger, so I took my time arranging the cookies and cupcakes on the silver platters while she walked into the other room."

"And you could still hear her?"

"Yes, Penny loves loud phone conversations."

"So you heard what they talked about?"

"Yes and no."

"What does that mean?"

"She loves loud phone conversations, and she loves watching reality shows."

"And?"

"And she loves loud phone conversations *while* watching loud reality TV shows."

"And? Can you tell me what you heard, at anything other than molasses speed?"

"Well, I heard Penny, and I heard the TV show."

"Are you telling me you couldn't tell the difference?"

Aurora shrugged. "Penny lived in Georgia for a few years, and she has a slight Southern twang."

She stopped, waiting for me to make a connection. I didn't.

"The show in the background was the *Housewives of Georgia*."

"What did you hear? Surely you can distinguish between real life and reality TV." But even as I said the words, I thought about how much that might not be true, especially given the drama in Bay Isles over the last few months.

"I heard a lot about a tumultuous relationship."

"Whose?" This pinged my interest.

Aurora scratched her cheek and twisted her lips back and forth to each side. A sign I've come to know. She's either about to lie or doesn't know the answer.

"Well, was it about Lucy and Clay or Penny and her husband? Or someone else?" I tapped my fingers against the wood tabletop.

"Penny was saying that her marriage to him was a fake?" Aurora blurted out.

"Whose marriage, hers?"

"No, maybe they were talking about someone else altogether. Because Penny said she was happily married, but no one better go wake that bear unless they wanted to be bit."

"That would mean; it's not Penny."

"Well, but then Penny said something like she was only there for the decoration most days."

"Could be trouble in paradise or just normal matrimony," I said.

Bales placed two drinks and a plate of sweets in front of us.

"Thank you." I nodded and grabbed a blueberry muffin, giving silent thanks that I was blessed with a high metabolism and the energy to run on the beach most mornings. This morning I had slept in. I didn't have the energy after my late night, but mostly after my meeting with Drew.

"She has a shaky alibi," Aurora said between bites of a peach scone.

"Shaky?"

"She was there at the park—"

"Half of the citizens of Bay Isles were there."

"Except you. You were at the police station." A strange, clouded look crossed Aurora's face.

"Thank goodness. But supposedly, so was the victim. Jerry must have hightailed it back to the park. He was released before me because he complained he had a job to do. He said he was missing an important interview, something he'd been working on for ten years."

That cloud passed over Aurora's eyes again. "Did you find out who he was interviewing?"

"No. The newspaper editor hasn't returned my calls. I heard the police confiscated his laptop, but Drew isn't talking about the case," I fibbed, between bites of the warm muffin. I wanted to wait until the right time to ask Aurora about her dad's business. But first, I wanted to hear about Penny.

"What was shaky about Penny's alibi?" I asked.

"No one saw her for about 15 to 20 minutes. Even her kids were looking for her."

"It's a big park. Any ideas where she went?"

"She claims she walked Gucci to the beach and to stick her feet in the water to cool off."

"Did anyone see her?"

"Nope. But then again, I haven't heard who saw who that day, including the victim."

"It's driving me nuts that we have no one to point at. In my gut, I don't think Penny killed Jerry, but I can't really prove she's innocent either. I know the police are interviewing everyone who was at the park and cross-referencing. Then they'll look at the physical evidence to rule out people, but I don't have any of that." I sighed. My thoughts went to my conversation with Drew last night, and a lump in my throat formed.

"Are you okay?" Aurora had a sad look in her eyes, but there was something else.

"Yes, I, um, I guess I'm just tired." I couldn't tell Aurora about last night. How could I explain my encounter with Tommy and then Drew? And the shoe! And now it and my bag were missing. I planned to give it to Drew before dinner tonight when he came over to search the Sea Ray. Now what was I going to do?

"Honestly, I don't know how you do it," Aurora said.

"Do what?"

"You own your own business, and you spend all this time helping the police. Why?"

"They need help." I shrugged.

"It seems more than that. I guess I worry that you can't let go."

"You mean I can't let go of what happened with my dad?"

"I'm not very subtle, am I?" Aurora stirred her coffee with an emerald green swizzle stick.

"It's true. I came here to open a business, but I also wanted answers, and clearly, my mom didn't know anything. So I moved here. I thought by being in Bay Isles, the last place my dad was seen before he went on the fateful mission, I could get answers. And I'm sorry if I spend all my spare time helping the deputies."

"You don't have to get involved."

"I can't help it."

"I'm your good friend but also your partner in the business. I'm okay with you taking time off, especially if it's helping you work through the loss of your dad. But I worry about you, Mo. You have to let the police do their thing. But I understand why you do this." Aurora placed her warm hand on mine.

I nodded and felt tears glisten in my eyes. "I guess if the authorities couldn't find my dad, or his killers, and bring them to justice, then I felt compelled to help find killers and bring closure to other families. It's a way of healing over his loss."

"But Mo, if you can't stop yourself from getting involved in police business, then you're not healing."

Aurora had a point, but why was she so insistent on me not helping Drew with this case? Maybe she was right; I shouldn't get involved.

"Part of healing is confronting the truth. And without knowing the truth about where my dad went missing and who killed him, then there will always be questions tethered to my past. I may never know what happened or who killed my dad. And I'll never have that closure. I get that. But that's why I feel so compelled to give that closure to others."

"You don't owe anything to Penny Jackson, or anyone for that matter," Aurora said.

I scratched my neck and had a thought.

"Do you think Penny was talking about Lucy and Clay's marriage?"

"I'm not sure. I do know Lucy wouldn't want to upset Clay," Aurora said.

"He's a big man."

"And when he's upset, let's just say you don't want to be around him. He was yelling at Lucy when she was here a week ago. Not only could he eat her for breakfast, but she'd barely have enough substance to fill the gaps between his teeth."

"What were they fighting about?" I was curious about Lucy since I wasn't convinced about the story she gave at the park when Penny found the body.

"He said she was hiding something from him."

"Like a secret or an object?"

"I got the impression it was an item because he asked if she had it hidden at the beach house." Aurora rubbed her chin, then pushed her bobbed hair behind her ears. "It was a notebook, I think. Or maybe he said journal."

"Hmmm. Did anyone else hear them?"

"The other café diners purposely ignored the two of them."

"Meaning they were all very aware of the disturbance in their otherwise refined world."

"Yup. He stormed outside, and Penny followed suit, so we never got to hear who won the fight."

"Forget who won. I just want to know what she could be hiding from her husband."

"Do you think it has to do with that reporter?"

"Could be. Think hard — did he say journal or notebook?" I asked Aurora.

"Neither," Bales' voice said from behind me.

I turned to see Bales standing next to our table.

"What?" I said.

"I didn't mean to eavesdrop, but working as a barista, I have fine-tuned my listening skills, so I hear a lot," Bales said.

"Like a bartender?"

"Yeah, you can say that. I can hear a conversation through the grinding, banging, pounding, humming, gurgling, and whistling." Bales laughed.

"Did you hear them argue too?" I took a sip of coffee.

"Aurora was halfway right. It was a journal of sorts."

I narrowed my eyes and twisted my mouth.

"A logbook," Bales said.

"A logbook?" I repeated.

"Yeah, like a record of daily business transactions," Bales

said. "He owns a lawn care and maintenance company, and he was accusing her of stealing the books."

"His business records? That's strange." But it had my mind buzzing. "Since they're married, are you sure he didn't mean their personal account statements?"

"Nope. I knew he was talking about his lawn care because I remember his truck out front. You know, the one with the funny logo?" Bales walked over to stand next to Aurora.

"The one that looks like the Law and Order logo? But it says Lawn and Order, SGU. Special Grass Unit. I love that logo," Aurora replied.

"Yes. I overheard him specifically say the LAO logbook was missing," Bales said.

"Lawn and Order," I said in a quiet voice. "I still can't imagine why he would think his wife would have it."

"She does his books, or her friend Penny does. I think Lucy has an accounting degree but has Penny help with the business tax stuff. I know this because Lucy brings her laptop in here a lot and works at that corner table while her kids are at school." Bales pointed to the small table tucked in the northeast corner of the café.

Even though the table was quite a distance from the front door and the farthest from other diners, it was close enough to the kitchen that Bales could easily eavesdrop.

"Is that where he was sitting when their fight broke out?" I needed to ask questions without having Bales, or Aurora, for that matter, suspect Lucy of anything other than a marital dispute.

"Yes. I suspected that he thought she cooked the books."

"Cooked the books or stole the books?" Aurora asked.

"Or misplaced the books," I added. "Why would she do that to her husband?" My stomach growled, and I reached over for another muffin. It was one of several perks of owning a café. I ate well. Both Aurora and Bales were excellent chefs. Aurora was a pastry chef who could dish up masterpieces. And Bales made the best sandwich concoctions you'd ever taste.

Bales shrugged.

Aurora excitedly chimed in. "She once left her notebook here."

"Lucy?" I was shocked. Why wouldn't Aurora have mentioned this before?

"Yeah. I see her here from time to time, too, and when she doesn't have a PC, she uses this battered notebook. When she left it behind, I took a peek in it and couldn't tell anything other than some scrawl of letters and numbers. She has abysmal penmanship."

My heart raced when I realized what Aurora might have seen. "Were they long numbers and an occasional letter?"

"Yeah, I guess you could say that. It was a plethora of numbers, some looked like temperatures, and maybe wind speeds. I just assumed they were for the Lawn and Order business."

My mind was racing. What if these numbers were latitudes and longitudes? I wanted to keep Aurora and Bales away from accusatory suspicions, so I trod lightly with my next couple of questions.

"It probably had to do with surveying. I heard his lawn care company surveyed plots occasionally."

Aurora nodded, but her mind seemed to be wandering. "They do Granny's yard work, too, right?"

"Jet is Granny's gardener and keeps all the potted plants in order. Still, Lucy's husband's lawn care company does the grounds. They mow, hedge, get rid of weeds, trim the palm fronds — that type of stuff. Why?"

"I don't know," Aurora said. "I remember seeing one of his trucks at the festival too."

"That's right. I did too. But there were a lot of locals there." I tried to think of something constructive to ask while I had both of my baristas here chatting but came up with nothing.

"Yup. Half the town was there."

That was the problem.

Aurora nodded and bit her lower lip.

My thoughts and concerns were interrupted by the café door swinging open.

Deputy Lucky and Deputy Cross entered.

Drew gave Aurora and me a glance, and then his face blushed.

Ruh-roh. I'd seen that look before. It was usually when he was writing tickets or arresting someone.

Drew was all business when he walked up to our table.

"Good morning, ladies," Drew said, without a smile in my direction, his eyes focused on Aurora.

Aurora looked at me, then Drew. "Good morning, deputies. Can we get you the usual?"

Deputy Cross started to say, "Sure—" but Drew interrupted him.

"Not this morning. We need to talk to Aurora. Will you join us at the station to answer a few questions?" Drew looked at Aurora and avoided me.

There was a chilly pause.

"Yes, of course," she said, in an awkward voice. "Let me get my purse."

This was not good. Blushing gave Drew away every time.

Aurora stood up and gave me a shy glance and a shrug over her shoulder as she trailed to the office to grab her handbag. Deputy Cross followed her.

I nodded toward the front door and followed Drew out on the porch, away from every ear in the café.

"Drew, what's going on? Can you ask her the questions here?"

"I need to speak with her privately."

"So you're going to haul her to the station in Palma County?" The Palma County deputies had jurisdiction over both Bay Isles and a neighboring town, Bridgeport. The sheriff's offices were on the outskirts of town. A place I knew all too well.

"As you probably already know from talking to Christine, initially the ME said Jerry was killed by the knife wound, but instead, he died from a blow to the head."

"I don't understand what that has to do with Aurora."

"Mo, Aurora gave us permission to search her place."

"Okay."

"Well, we're probably going to arrest her."

"For what? For making a bad cup of coffee?" I hated my attempt at humor at a serious time like this.

"For extortion. And for suspicion of murder."

"Drew, are you kidding me?" My mouth was dry. I felt worse than I did last year when he threatened to arrest me. "How can you do that? On what grounds?"

"Based on the evidence."

"What evidence?"

"The evidence we found at her apartment and in the victim's hotel room."

"What?"

"We found Aurora's fingerprints on the serrated knife that was used to stab Jerry. And that same knife found at the scene was from her set of knives at her home."

"But everyone touched the knife at the park. It was used to slice pies." I couldn't believe Drew would think Aurora could hurt a fly. I felt sick.

"We have to deduce that whoever used the knife really

wanted him dead and decided to use a blunt object to clobber him as well."

I rubbed my hand over my mouth. But why Aurora? "Someone is setting her up. Why would she want Jerry Ryder—"

"— there's more." Drew touched my arm.

I sucked in a deep breath. "You said extortion. What does that mean?"

"She wrote threatening letters to Jerry," Drew said.

I shook my head. "I just don't believe it."

"Her dad's business was facing bankruptcy."

"And you think Jerry was going to expose something about their business? You have little evidence. And from what I've heard, Jerry made a lot of enemies from his articles." But I remembered what Drew had said the night before about the slander lawsuit.

We were interrupted by Deputy Cross, leading Aurora out of the café.

"Wait," I yelled. "Aurora, wait."

But Deputy Cross had put her in the patrol car.

I turned to Drew. "I can't believe you. I can't believe you think she did anything. Tell her I'll call her dad to get her a lawyer," I said quietly.

Drew left without uttering another word.

CHAPTER NINETEEN

After the patrol car pulled away, I returned to the café.
The nervous chatter and excitement had reached maximum volume, but when I re-entered the café, the room quieted, and the crowd around the counters parted for me like I was Molly Moses commanding the Red Sea.

I walked quickly to my office and shut the door to drown out the gossiping. I sat in my chair and placed my head in my hands.

I sat at my desk a few minutes, taking deep breaths.

There was a light tap on my door.

"Who is it?"

"Hey Molly, it's Bales."

I opened the door. "What's up?"

She looked at me with sympathetic eyes. "Your ten o'clock appointment is here."

I scratched my eyebrow. "My appointment?"

"Yes. Penny Jackson is here."

"Penny?" Then it hit me. She had set up a meeting with me in the park a few days earlier, before the murder.

"Yes. Do you want her to come back to the office, or are you coming out?" Bales said softly.

"Can you have her come back here? Give me a few minutes," I instructed.

"Ok. Can I bring you anything to drink?"

"No. Thank you."

Bales shut the door.

Now, here in my office, I had a decision to make. I could either trust that Drew and his deputies would figure out who killed Jerry Ryder, or I could break the rules again and investigate the crime myself. My sleuthing had gotten me results in the past. Why not now?

Let's face it, I had been fiddling around in the investigation from the beginning. But now I was all in. My best friend was counting on it. It was one thing to snoop around and ask questions of strangers, but it was another thing entirely to start interviewing potential suspects. And Penny was on the suspect list.

There was no way I had faith in the new deputy. I had done some investigation on my own regarding Deputy Cross. And I had found out that he was a gullible gumshoe and had a propensity for arresting the wrong suspects.

He's a dimwit detective, Christine had told me a few days ago. And *he had a bad habit of arresting the wrong suspects based on hunches*. If it had been up to Deputy Drew Powell, Aurora would not be at the station.

I made my choice.

Penny came in wearing a pair of jeans and a light blue tank top. She managed to look casual, almost disheveled, but in an interesting, expensive way, like a billboard ad for Ralph Lauren.

She eyed my tiny office and then looked like she was going to make a snide remark but paused and nodded.

"Hi Molly." Penny's ruby red lips were pursed and were a stark contrast to her pale skin.

"Hi Penny," I replied. "Did Bales get you a cold chai tea latte with a raspberry drizzle?"

She nodded and held up a tall, clear plastic glass covered with condensation.

"Good. Have a seat, or would you rather talk in the café? I know it's cramped in here."

"No, this is fine. I only have a few minutes." Penny pulled out the other chair in my office and sat across from me. "And the privacy is good."

I nodded. "How've you been?"

"I'm fine now." Sincere sorrow flashed across her face, indicating to me she wasn't likely to have been involved in Jerry's death, or something else was bothering her. It took her a lot of courage to come here.

"Have the police let up?"

"It was ruthless at first. I was the one who found the body. Naturally, I'm the one they'd suspect. I didn't even know the reporter," she said, with an edge in her voice.

This gave me an opening. "I know you didn't come here to discuss the murder. But if you don't mind me asking, who do you think did it?"

Penny shot me a look that clearly was meant to admonish me for asking her the same question the police had.

"I don't know. At first, I had no doubt it was the kitchen knife in his neck that killed him. But then I'd been at the police station for five hours, you know, right after I found the body."

"Being interrogated?"

"Yes. It was awful. But they left me alone a few times. They were on defcon. It was like they were dealing with a tidal wave at the police station."

"I bet." I smiled.

She relaxed. "The first time Deputy Cross left, he said he needed to get some forms. I just sat in that quiet so-called interrogation room alone. The second time was five hours and 15 minutes in; he left to relieve himself. My lawyer, Pat Bostwick, was there then, but he got up and left after Deputy Cross. That's when I read the file upside down."

Penny talked about a few items in the report that I already knew. Time of death. Place of death. Cause of death.

"And what was the ME's official cause?" I asked, curiosity piqued.

"It mentioned a blow to the head." She shook her head like she was trying to escape the fresh pictures in her mind. "I remember, all too well, the darkened, matted hair of the head wound. But I just thought he fell on a rock."

"Do you recall a puddle of blood by his head? And did the police find a rock nearby?"

"No, but the report said the ME thought he was bashed on the back of the head."

"It appears whoever wanted him dead wanted to make sure he didn't survive the stabbing assault." I knew enough about murders to know when it was personal or not, so I had to ask Penny the next question. "Could you tell by looking at him if it was multiple blows?"

"No. But the report...." She trailed off and stared at a spot behind me on the wall, and she turned as pale as a coed on the first day of spring break.

"What did it say?"

"The stab wound was from a left-handed person. I'm right-handed."

"Uh-huh," I said, my eyes fixed on Penny.

"But the blow was, well, from a right-handed person."

"What?"

"It was confusing. I've never read a police file. And I was afraid my attorney would come back in. I could see him right outside the door, talking."

"What else?"

"It had a lot of shorthand notes, but what I surmised was that he really hadn't bled a lot from the head wound, and supposedly, the indent in his skull was clearly visible."

I put my hand to my mouth. The blow made it personal. "Indent?"

"The bash was so hard it had left a distinct impression on Jerry's skull. An imprint that didn't match a rock."

"Did it say what made the impression?" For the hundredth time since Jerry's death, I wished I had access to the police records.

"It doesn't make sense."

"What doesn't make sense?"

"The impression."

"What was it?" My bet was on an anchor.

"It was round, with curved edges, and had a seam that left a craterlike depression."

I gave Penny a look that said, *What was it*?

"The impression matched a cannonball."

"A what?"

She took a sip of her drink. "A cannonball. Like for the reenactment."

I nodded. "Was it shot at him? Or was he cracked over the head? "

"Smacked on the head."

"Why doesn't it make sense? Everything from cannonballs to horses to fodder had to be rented for the festival. I'm sure there was one lying around." But as I said the words, I didn't believe them.

"Not according to the notes in the file. The vendors hadn't set up yet."

"Where did it come from?" Suddenly, I was more curious about why Penny would take the risk of reading the file. I had my doubts about her being the murderer, but those were now fading.

"The file showed them interviewing the vendors, but none were missing any supplies." Then Penny dismissed it with a wave of her hand. "It doesn't matter that much to me. I heard they have someone else to focus on."

Aurora? I thought. *What does Penny know?*

"What? Are you saying that they have another suspect?"

"Come on, Molly. You know they're questioning Aurora. What I can't understand is *why*."

Should I tell her about the fingerprints? I definitely wouldn't tell her about Aurora's threatening letters to the deceased.

I nodded solemnly, trying not to look obvious on my answer. "Yeah, I heard."

"You know a lot more than you're saying. And I understand. I'm not asking you about Aurora. Everyone hated that guy. Who do you think did him in?"

I shrugged, not wholly trusting Penny. Maybe it was time to change the subject.

"Why did you asked to meet?" I recalled that Penny had set up this meeting before they found Jerry's body. She had my curiosity piqued.

"Well, so much for murder talk," Penny said.

"Come on, Penny, what do you want from me? I'm not good at this let's-be-friends thing."

"I know. Me neither. The funny thing is, Molly, at a different time, we might have been friends. Maybe when you marry that deputy guy of yours and have kids, we could be friends."

"Sure, PTA buddies." I grinned.

Penny laughed and reached into her purse and pulled out a notebook. She looked at me for a fleeting second as if she couldn't believe she was even considering talking to me about something that left a worried look on her face.

"When we were at the park, I mentioned I had something to talk to you about." She cleared her throat. "You know I keep the books for several businesses."

"Yes. I heard that." Did she want to solicit my café as a client?

"I'm not a forensic accountant or fraud investigator, but when I see something that doesn't jive, it always piques my interest."

"I'm not following you."

She shifted in her chair. "Look, I didn't have anyone to talk to about this. And I know you and your deputy boyfriend might be curious about this." She turned to a page in her notebook, and there was a small slip of paper folded in a square. She handed it to me.

I cocked my head and accepted the paper and glanced over at Penny, who was watching me with interest.

"Go ahead and read it," she said.

I unfolded the paper that looked like it had been folded and unfolded many times. It had hanging bits of paper on the spiral-bound side where it had been torn out. I looked closely, and there was a string of numbers written in blue ink. The numbers appeared similar to the ones I had seen a few days earlier.

"What's this?" I asked, pretending I didn't know they were latitudes and longitudes. "And where did you get this?"

"Well, this is between you and me. And if you share it with your deputy friend, I'd use discretion."

"Who gave you this?" I repeated.

"I do the books for Lawn and Order, and a week ago, Lucy brought over three boxes so I could work on filing their tax return that's due in a few weeks. And while digging through a stack of receipts, I found this." She tapped the paper sitting on the desk. "These are specific coordinates of locations on the water."

"So Clay kept track of his fishing spots. That's not uncommon," I said.

"But Clay doesn't fish." Penny bit her lower lip. "I think these are locations of the stolen boats."

I struggled not to sigh. "Hmmm," I said, trying to digest this. "Why do you think this has anything to do with the stolen boats?" Even as I looked at the numbers, I wondered if they matched the ones Drew had. Then it occurred to me. *What if these are from Drew's field notebook?*

Penny's expression shifted from a flash of concern and she shook her head. "Well, geez, Molly. I have gone this far. I might as well tell you what I know. What do I have to lose? I mean, you really don't think I killed that reporter?"

How did I answer that? I'd like to believe Penny, but I couldn't trust her. Plus, I was more concerned about the amount of evidence against Aurora. And until the killer was caught, Aurora would have that black cloud following her. Anything Penny had to share could be helpful.

"What do you have?"

Penny reached into her purse and pulled out a file folder. "The LAO books don't make sense."

"Whose books?" I reached for the manila file folder, but Penny put a protective hand on it.

"Don't you see? Lucy always wears expensive clothes, and her kids go to a private school."

"So I assume there's good money in lawn care."

"I suppose there is. But not Clay's. He's a gambler. He spends more than he makes. And I've been doing their books for years. They've lost a lot of business, and yet their bank account keeps growing."

"And you think what? He's stealing boats?" I asked, connecting the dots. I tried to look mortified, even though I didn't care for Lucy's husband much. He was as crooked as a fishhook.

"He has a lot of connections to Mexico. And these boats keep going missing. And his account keeps growing."

"Connections?"

Her eyes widened, and her skin looked paler. "He recruits families from Mexico for his lawn business. As his accountant, I know he travels south a few times a year."

I rubbed my chin. "This is a tough accusation, especially coming from a murder suspect."

She stared at me with a look like she was being trapped. "Come on, Mo, I didn't kill Jerry. Why would I leave the murder weapon with my fingerprints on it at the park? And then find the body? If I had anything to do with this, I wouldn't have left that knife in his throat."

She had a point. But was the knife the actual murder weapon, or was it the blow that killed Jerry?

"Do you have any other evidence of the boat crimes besides this piece of paper and bad spending habits?"

Penny took a sip of her cold brew. She shook her plastic cup, and we both watched the ice swirl in the red liquid. "No. That's why I came to see you. I figured if the police find the boat thieves, they can focus more on solving the murder."

I swallowed. "Who else knows about this?"

"No one. Lucy is my only friend. I can't tell her."

I nodded. I knew instinctively that Aurora was not the murderer. But I couldn't tell about Penny's involvement. I was also wary of her reluctance to get involved in the investigation. "Why not take this theory to the police?"

"I'm afraid I might lose my friend. I know accusing someone of stealing boats can tarnish a friendship. I can't believe Lucy would have anything to do with this, but what are these numbers for?"

I actually felt sorry for Penny. I was going through a similar quandary with Aurora. I had a piece of evidence that I had been holding on to that could be damaging to Aurora. The tortoise-shell-colored comb that Aurora had worn the day of the festival had little rhinestones on it, similar to the one I had found wedged in my palm on the path to the beach. I didn't want to take it to the police until I had more proof. Absentmindedly, I rubbed my bruised wrist.

"Plus, I don't want Lucy to find out. Clay Lavender is six-foot-three and two hundred pounds of pure badass when he's teed off," Penny said. "Lucy always said she walks the chalk when she's around him."

"And sounds like you do too. Besides this paper and the books, what else do you have?" I tried to suppress my growing frustration, knowing that patience would fare better than snippiness and doubt in this situation.

"Can you help find the murder weapon?"

"The cannonball?"

"Yup. Since the police have the knife with my fingerprints on it already, what about the other weapon?" Penny said, standing up and placing the folder and notebook in her purse. "What happened to that?"

The thought did occur to me that the police were searching Aurora's apartment for more than her kitchen knife set. But this fact was safe with me.

"I agree it's worth a shot. But I think finding a loose cannonball would be like finding a needle in a haystack if we just knew what haystacks to search." Even though I hadn't meant for Penny to know I would interfere with Drew's investigation, just hearing that there were still options out there besides Aurora as the primary suspect took a load off my shoulders.

I desperately wanted to locate the murder weapon, but

another theory kept running amok in my mind, and I wasn't ready to share it with anyone just yet.

CHAPTER TWENTY

I couldn't wait to start working on the case. But with Aurora at the police station, I needed to first help Bales out in the cafe.

There was no denying the wonderful appeal of baking and working at the café. Making drinks for customers was a part of my work that didn't feel like a job. How many people got to say they baked and sold sweets and beverages and delivered something that made people smile?

I had slipped a cardboard java jacket onto the paper cup of Americano when I stopped to watch a group of seniors who were gathered in the west corner of the café enjoying a weekly book club session. One smiled sweetly at me as she walked to the restroom with her cane. All of the other eyes on me looked worried.

Bales caught their stares and whispered to me, "You're always going to be the sleuth barista who solves murders."

I cracked the bakery drawer open, and a puff of sweetly scented air escaped. I placed a pistachio muffin on a plate then turned to Bales. "I'm sure they've heard about Aurora. I mean, after all, gossiping is the favorite pastime around here besides fishing."

Bales smiled. "They're probably all wondering what you're going to do about it, especially since you date a deputy."

I snapped a lid on the coffee cup and lowered my voice. "Drew has to do his job, and he can't show any bias."

"But that shouldn't preclude you from helping out like you did a few months ago. If anyone can ferret out clues, it's you. And besides, gossip has it that the new deputy who took Aurora away is as dumb as a sack of hammers."

"And gossip is gospel in this town."

"Well, I saw it firsthand. Deputy Cross was in here a few days ago. He didn't know how to use his iPhone."

"Not the vote of confidence you'd expect in a new deputy." Maybe Bales was right. My stomach tingled with nerves.

"Go. Do what you need to do. Ericka and I can handle it today. And I can call Granny Dee to come in and help with the baking and food prep."

"She had a lunch date with Timothy." Granny Dee had a so-called suitor, Timothy Carlin. He was a retired, full-time snowbird and a transplant from New York. He was kind enough and adored Granny.

"We've got this, Mo. Go help Aurora." Bales took the Americano and muffin plate out of my hands and walked around the counter to a waiting customer sitting at a table.

I tugged off the apron and plastic gloves I was wearing.

Bales returned and said, "Your tribe is in good hands. Now shoo. I have baking to do."

"Don't get carried away. I'll be back before you all can burn the place down," I said as I turned and walked in the kitchen.

My cell phone vibrated in my pocket. It was a text from Tommy. ***Call me. It's urgent.***

I stood behind the stainless-steel door and called Tom.

He answered on the first ring.

"What's up?" I said.

He was hysterical. "She's gone! Kathy's gone!"

"She left you?" I wanted to pull back the words as soon as I said them.

He calmed down enough to reply. "No. She had left last night when I got back. She left me a note. She said she didn't mean to do it, and she needed to go talk to someone."

"Do what?"

"I don't know, Molly. She hasn't been herself for the last few days. Ever since she got back from the festival." He sniffled and mumbled something incoherent.

"Wait. Calm down, Tom, try to breathe. Did you look for her? Is there anywhere she could go?"

"I've been looking since I found the note. I told the police." There was a pause as Tom took some deep breaths. "Those deputies are useless."

"Have you checked her credit cards?" I hated to say it, but I assumed she went home. She was upset at Tommy the last time I saw her.

"That's the thing. Her clothes and suitcases are here at the hotel. And her credit cards haven't been used."

"Does she have cash for a taxi?"

"I suppose she has some cash." Tom swore.

"Did you argue yesterday?" I asked through gritted teeth.

"She — she told me she was scared of something she did," he said, sadness enveloping his voice.

"Scared?"

"I didn't pay that much attention, and I wanted to get away from the arguing. That's when I left for the bars. I drank a lot yesterday. And then I went out boating. The last text I got from her was late last night."

"This isn't your fault," I said. Or maybe it was?

Tom took a deep breath. "It's not that easy, you know? She's been acting strange ever since we got here. And it isn't about you and me. It's something different from her past."

"Where are you?"

"I'm back at the hotel. Mo, I haven't slept. She doesn't know anyone here. Where would she go?"

I thought I knew. "Let me call you back. Give me a few hours."

I was about to hang up, and Tommy said, "Oh Mo, you still there?"

"Yup."

"You asked me about Kathy's white tennis shoes."

"Yes," I said apprehensively.

"She said she was missing one. Is that a coincidence? She said she thought she packed a pair but was cursing about how she must have left one at home."

"That sounds like Kathy. Absentminded as usual."

I hung up and went to my office in search of my backpack.

As I walked out the back door of the café, I let out a low whistle. Snickers came running from somewhere over by the beach. I clicked my tongue twice, and Snickers sat at my heels.

I bent down and attached his leash. "Sorry, pal. We have to pretend we're going for a walk. You know the routine: You get loose, and I search the yards, fields, garages, and anywhere I need to look for you."

This worked most of the time.

It had been an hour since I spoke to Tommy, and I hadn't found one clue. I'd been searching backyards, boathouses, garages (that didn't involve breaking in and entry). All this couldn't wait until dark. I had spent the last few hours hunting down my theory, and I was running out of time.

Aurora was still detained at the police station. Kathy was missing. Penny was on a quest for evidence and weapons. Bales and Granny were holding down the fort at my café. Tommy was searching for Kathy. Drew had a secret relationship with a female named Monica, that he wasn't telling me about yet. What a hot mess.

I had to search for the evidence for Aurora's sake, but I was bewildered about the recent shenanigans and the whereabouts of Kathy.

I figured Kathy just left town. She had to be high up on Deputy Drew's suspect list too. When Drew came over to Granny's in a few hours to search the Sea Ray, I would come clean. I would tell him everything. I would show him the pieces of rhinestones from Aurora's hair comb, even though that could put her on site close to the victim. I would tell him about the gloves and newspaper articles I saw in Kathy's handbag. I would tell him what Penny shared with me. I would tell him about the now-missing white tennis shoe.

But first, I needed to find a missing piece of the puzzle.

I peered into the business window and saw several workers sitting on folding chairs. I looked at Snickers.

"Let's do this. Go ahead and speak. Bark."

Snickers started barking furiously.

"I'll be back," I said to him. "Stay and bark."

Several workers looked over at the window and got up and moved toward the noise.

Just what I needed.

I slipped in the side door while they went out of the front door.

Within minutes, I was back by Snickers. "Oh, there you are," I said, as I came around and saw the crew petting Snickers.

I held up the leash. "He got unhooked. Sorry." I snapped Snickers' collar to the leash.

"No problemo," one said.

"Let's go," I said, as I pulled Snickers. When I turned my back to the three men, I smiled as big as I could.

———

I went to the boathouse and unlocked the Sea Ray. It was musty and covered with grit. I had a few minutes before Drew would arrive, so I decided to work my frustration out by cleaning the boat.

I grabbed a bucket.

Where was the marine soap and brush? I searched the racks behind the Yeti coolers. When I saw Granddad's Yetis, it hit me that I had to tell Drew about the items stolen from my SUP.

When I reached for the soap on the top shelf, I saw out of the corner of my eye a large pile of lawn trimmings, including palm fronds. *Why would Jet leave them in the boathouse?* I thought.

A flash of yellow fur peeked out at the bottom of the pile, causing a girlish scream to erupt from me. Since the fur hadn't moved, I assumed I would be dealing with a dead cat. How creepy.

"I'll wait until Drew gets here to help me move all this brush and deal with the dead stray." I stepped back from the pile.

I almost turned away when I noticed a brown leather strap sticking out of the opposite end of the pile.

On closer inspection, it wasn't a leather belt. It was a boot. And not just any boot, but a foot wearing a brown studded one. And there were two of them.

Oh no. No. No. No.

There had to be an explanation for what I was seeing. If I could uncover the cat, I could see that this was just a big pile of rubbish.

My shaky hand dug at the loose twigs around the yellow fur.

"Holy crap!" I resisted an urge to vomit as I stared at the waxy face of Kathy.

I struggled to keep my wobbly legs from giving out on me. "Crap!"

I looked closer and saw a small cord wrapped around her throat. The ends of the red rope were frazzled.

"Damn you, Kathy. Why did you have to turn up dead? And why are you here in my granddad's boathouse?"

As much as I hated to disturb the body, I wanted answers before Drew came waltzing in.

"Ohhh," I groaned. "Drew."

What was he going to say?

The dizziness didn't dissipate as I continued to search around the body and inspect the scene.

When I found the note in her pocket with my telephone number on it, I forced myself to breathe.

Do not scream. Do not faint.

A little drool had begun to run down my chin.

The air in the boathouse was stifling hot, and I needed fresh air

I ran outside and smacked into Deputy Drew. I fell against him, trembling from head to toe. He grasped my arm and helped steady me.

"Mo, are you okay?"

"I'm okay… Kathy."

"I know. There's still no word on her whereabouts. I talked to Tommy—"

"Nooo!" I cried and buried my face in his chest.

"Are you sure you're okay? You're shaking." Drew scrutinized my face, a worried look reflected in the crease of his brow. "Let's go inside."

"No," I managed to say.

"No, you don't want to go inside, or no, what? I think you're hyperventilating. Breathe, Mo."

I didn't know how to tell Drew, but there was no way around it. "It's just that I know where Kathy is."

"That's great. Why didn't you say so? Tom will get off my case. Where is she?"

I pointed toward the boathouse with a trembling finger.

His eyes looked first at the boathouse, then back at me.

"Mo? What is she doing in there?" His voice rose as he said "there" like he knew that she was not going to come walking out on her own.

"Oh Drew, I really don't know how she got there." My voice cracked.

"I think I understand," he blurted before he started running toward the boathouse.

I must have known the *finding-the-dead-body-routine* all too well because I sat on the back porch steps and dialed 9-1-1.

This was a job I needed to do sitting down.

A few minutes later, I entered Granny's kitchen. She looked at me with worry in her eyes.

"What in God's name is going on out there?" Granny said as she strained and lowered her eyes at me. Henrietta stood next to her.

"Why do you say that?" I said but realized I couldn't keep my eyes from bouncing back toward the boathouse. I looked over at Drew, and his jaw was set tight, and a worried look stayed on his face as he waited for the rest of the troops to show up.

"You might as well spit it out," Granny said, glancing at me then Drew. "It's clear as water that something is going on in the boathouse."

I had to hand it to the old gal. She could clearly see that Drew and I were straining for normalcy but not pulling it off.

Henrietta lowered her eyes and stared at me.

"I found Kathy."

"Found?"

"Yes. She's dead."

Granny gasped. Henrietta crossed herself.

"Oh no," Granny placed her hand over her mouth. "And you?"

"I'm fine. Not hurt."

"Oh dear. I love you, Mo, but you're going to give me a heart attack with all your meddling."

"Meddling? I just happened to stumble on bodies more than the normal person."

"You're a murder magnet."

"A what?"

"Murder seems to follow you everywhere."

———

Cops and EMTs peppered Granny's backyard within ten minutes, pushing me, Granny and Henrietta away from the body and corralling us on the back porch.

A flimsy line of yellow crime-scene tape was draped across the boathouse barn doors.

I had spent several minutes giving Drew my informal statement. I would have to go to the sheriff's office later to share everything I knew. It had been only four months since several of the deputies and Bay Isle citizens had considered me a possible murderer, and I could only imagine what they'd think of me finding another body. This time in Granny's garage!

My stomach lurched uncomfortably, knowing Kathy's lifeless body was lying in the boathouse. Even though I had no love lost for her, I certainly didn't wish her dead. My eyes pricked with fresh tears. She had been a friend once, and no matter what she had done, she didn't deserve to be strangled.

"Are you okay, Ms. Mo?" Henrietta asked, handing me a cup of tea.

I nodded.

Granny joined us outside. She had an old crocheted afghan wrapped around her. She stooped down next to me on the steps and swaddled part of the blanket around me. Henrietta sat on the other side of Granny and wrapped the other end of the throw around her.

Once again, there was drama at my doorstep. And a crime scene at Granny's home.

The three of us watched the flurry of lights and activity in the backyard. Small plastic green numbers were set on the grass and the ramp to the water for possible evidence collection and to trace all the tracks in and out of the boathouse. Kevin, the EMT, wheeled the metal gurney to the entrance of the garage.

Henrietta pressed the corner of the blanket to her eye. "Here we go again."

"Mo, dear, this isn't going to look good for you," Granny said. "You've been seen fighting with the dead woman, and some may think you were getting even with her for stealing your boyfriend."

I nodded and held in a string of curse words.

"You're a trouble magnet," Henrietta said.

"That seems to be my motto today. You all know I didn't strangle Kathy and then haul her body to hide it in Granny's boathouse," I whispered.

"Why do you think she was killed somewhere else?"

"There's no signs of struggle here and she has drag marks on her heels."

"But why leave her here?"

"Exactly. If I had killed her, I wouldn't leave her body in your garage."

"Yes, and now I want to know how you are going to prove you didn't do it," Granny murmured.

"Based on the feel and color of her skin, she's been dead a while. It was long enough for rigor to set in," I said.

Henrietta cleared her throat.

Granny coughed nervously.

"Someone is trying to frame me for the murder. I recognized the rope on her neck, and I bet if Drew searches my paddleboard, he'll see it's missing the leash I use for an anchor." I sighed. If word got out that I was a suspect in yet another murder, my café could be ruined. I could lose the Bean, and that was something I just couldn't take.

"And your fingerprints are probably on it." Granny squeezed my knee.

"Yeah. Lucky me." I watched Drew walk over to the three of us.

"Lucky you," Granny said.

"Can I speak with you?" He looked at me with tired eyes. "And you two ladies stay put; we'll need your statements."

"Oh, good grief," Granny said, frustrated. "You can't possibly think for one minute that Molly could have anything to do with that bitch, um, the dead person in there, can you?"

Drew raised his hands. "I'm not saying anything."

"Mo couldn't even lift Kathy," Henrietta said.

Drew sighed. "Well, the fact is, Kathy's body was found here. And I have to find out why. That's my job. So I need to document everything. That's why I need her at the station. I'll need both of your statements to find out if you heard or saw anything."

"Oh no, here we go again," Henrietta said, referring to when the three of us were suspects in a murder investigation last Christmas.

"Do we need to call the Mayor's brother?" Granny asked.

Mayor Clawson's brother was the town's lawyer and had assisted me last year.

"No, let's not call in lawyers yet. We need to document it and see where it goes."

I stood up, and when I did, Granny leaned over and whispered in my ear. "Mo, you know who did this. Now go put this case to rest."

I winked at her before turning toward Drew.

"Well, this conveniently points the finger at you," he said.

"I have a sealed-tight alibi for my whereabouts all day. With a ton of witnesses." I did have a few hours snooping that no one knew where I was. I needed the ME to narrow down the time.

"I was working all day at the café from early this morning until mid-day. It's not like I snuck out from waiting tables, killed Kathy, then threw her in my kayak and jetted down the Intracoastal canals to the boathouse in daylight without my café customers noticing my absence. So unless she was killed after four p.m., I don't see how I could be a suspect on this one."

I leaned forward and said softly to Drew, "Do you really think I would kill Kathy? Or anyone, for that matter?"

"Of course not. Is there anyone who wants to retaliate against you?" he asked.

I sighed. Where did I start? I knew one person who would want to pin Kathy's murder on me. But I didn't want to share my theory with Drew yet. "No. But, I have some thoughts."

I could see the tension in his posture.

"Anything you know that can help in my investigation, I need to know. I'm going to lose this case. Since the murder in the park has been unsolved, the state police are headed here to take it over."

Anger coursed through my body, and I stood up straighter. Given that Drew and his deputies had a long list of suspects and not enough proof to arrest anyone, it wasn't surprising the state police would get involved.

"That's crap," I said. My thoughts went to the odd conversation between Tommy and Kathy. Should I share their argument with Drew now? But I had not told Drew that I was once again sniffing around where I didn't belong. Why bring up the rum runner conversation now? And what would be Tommy's motive? He loved Kathy, didn't he?

Drew nodded, and his eyes looked sad. "Yeah, there's nothing I can do about it. Between the boat thieves, the reporter's murder, and now a second murder, my hands are tied." He abruptly stopped speaking and stared behind me.

His jaw clenched, and his gaze was fixed on something over my shoulder. I turned around to watch what looked like his black pickup truck pull up the driveway.

The headlights blinded me for a few seconds. Once the lights went dark, I recognized Drew's truck. What I didn't recognize next was the woman who stepped out from behind the steering wheel.

I stared in shock as a tall blonde stepped out and turned her cowboy boots in our direction.

CHAPTER TWENTY-ONE

Before the lady could get close to us, I backed up and fell into Drew. We both landed on the ground.

Within seconds, I was staring at a nice pair of alligator boots. When I stood up, on further inspection, she was a female version of Drew.

All sorts of scenarios ran through my mind.

"Hey there, beautiful," Deputy Drew said, standing up and shaking the boot girl's hand.

"Hey bro," she replied.

Bro?

"Molly, meet Paige. My sister." Drew gave me a sly grin. "Paige Powell, this is Molly Brewster."

"Paige? Sister?" I let out a deep sigh and breath I wasn't aware I was even holding.

"You look a bit relieved," Paige said. "Nice to meet you."

"I...well, it's just that...I thought you..." I stuttered.

Paige looked like she was trying hard not to giggle.

"Paige, or Monica as she's known here, has been helping me with the boat thieves' case."

I knew Drew had a sister, Paige, from Texas, but he never told me she was a detective too.

"Paige is a cop?" I asked softly. "And her name isn't even Monica?"

He nodded.

"Geez, where are my manners? Nice to meet you." I reached over to hug her. "I never saw that coming."

"Nice to finally meet you too." Paige gave me a small smile. "Drew called me a few days ago. I had a vacation planned and while I was here, why not help out?"

"She's being modest. Paige is the best undercover Ranger in Texas. She and I worked together undercover on a similar case in Laredo, a small town south of the Texas border, before I came to Palma County. She's as good as they come. Sorry I couldn't introduce her properly." Drew glanced over at the deputies securing the crime scene.

"I understand." But deep down, I had wished Drew would have given me a straight answer earlier. "What have you found out?" I wondered if she knew what I found out earlier today.

Paige looked at Drew, visibly trying to hold back words.

"Nothing you need to know at the moment," Drew said.

Paige exhaled and nodded. "Sorry, Molly. We're close, so please keep my relationship to Drew quiet right now. It's important to this case," Paige said.

"Of course." I wanted answers, but I wasn't getting very far.

Drew looked around, clearly uncomfortable with the three of us chatting, which made sense. Why would I have hugged Detective Monica? And this was probably why he shook her hand.

To stay in the undercover game, I said loudly, "You can take my statement at the station when my attorney is present."

Several lingering EMTs glanced our way but went back to their business.

"What do you know about this?" Paige asked, pointing toward the boathouse, a slight grin on her face.

"Drew has my statement. But I found Kathy around six pm. Rigor puts her time of death a lot earlier. And I have alibis."

"With witnesses of her whereabouts," Drew added.

Paige nodded. She seemed to accept this premise, so I continued to discuss what I had found. I began to wonder if I was heading in a direction that would pull me deeper into something I might not be able to get out of. That question rolled around uncomfortably in my mind for about three seconds.

"The murder weapon is still wrapped around her neck. It's a not the common rope that most paddleboarders or kayakers use. It's a smaller grade than used on a boat. Not as heavy, and well, it's a dog leash."

Paige tilted her head, then bent over and reached into her cowboy boot and pulled out a small notepad.

"I like a pair of alligator boots that can also work as a handbag," I said. "Just don't tell me you have a pistol in there too."

"A small one," she said.

"But a large knife." Drew smiled.

Paige opened the notebook and used a small pencil attached to jot down notes. "A leash?"

I nodded. "You'll notice the red stains around her ankles under her boots," I said.

"And I suppose she wasn't carrying a red moleskin notebook to cause the stains." Paige had a beautiful smile. "What do you think it's from?" she asked. Her pale blue eyes matched Drew's. Paige's long hair looked good on her. Not like the extensions Kathy wore.

"Silk Cotton Tree, also known as the Kapok. It produces pods full of cotton fiber with seeds embedded in it — a rare tree. Not too many in our area that are that mature. The adult tree produces hundreds of these huge 15-inch seed pods. Its large red flowers can cause a stain. I'm sure the ME will know this too."

"But he's pretty backed up. It may take him a few days for a full report," Drew said.

"She's smart, and she's beautiful," Paige said to Drew, then turned to me. "What else do you have?"

"When I got to the boathouse this evening, I couldn't even make out the water behind it. The bulging mangroves have grown so tall, and they're butted up against the low-lying brown-skirted palm trees, which make a thick wall of vegetation blocking out the water views and preventing a straight path for carrying or dragging a body," I said. *But a trailer could do it,* I thought. "Her boot heels are surprisingly clean, but the floor isn't," I added.

"So someone either wiped them off…" Paige said.

"…Or she wasn't dragged," Drew added.

I nodded. And based on Kathy's frame and weight, I couldn't have carried her body alone. Not many people could.

Both turned and looked at me like "anything else?"

"And she's not wearing her engagement ring," I said with the final blow that I knew somehow would point directly at me as a suspect.

"She's not?" Drew asked.

"No, she is not. So the question is why would she flaunt her ring all around my café the other day for the world to see that she was engaged to my ex-boyfriend, and then go out for the day without wearing it?" I thought I knew the answer, but I wondered if Drew or his sister would. I also knew the ring would not be back at her hotel.

"Yeah, I'd agree, most newly engaged women never take their ring off," Paige said. "We can check her hotel."

I frowned.

"What do you think happened to it?" Drew asked curiously.

"I think I know. But I need a few hours to check out a theory," I said.

Drew glanced at Paige. "See, I told you. She's always interfering in my investigations."

"Only the cases that point to me or my friends and family as suspects," I added.

"And I hear that happens a lot," Paige said.

We were interrupted by Deputy Cross walking up to us. He blushed when he looked at Paige. "Hi Detective Dell," he said. "Can I have a word with you? Or do you need to stay to hear Mo, um, I mean, Ms. Brewster's statement?" He blushed deeper red.

"Monica Dell," Drew whispered to me.

I nodded.

"Go ahead. I'll catch up in a few," Drew said to Paige.

When Paige and Deputy Cross walked away, I turned to Drew. "Dell? Monica Dell?"

"I couldn't use Powell. She couldn't have the same last name as me."

"Of course not, but Dell?"

"What can I say? I was using my EliteBook PC, so Dell was the first name that came to mind on the request form for her undercover name."

"Seriously?"

He shrugged.

"HP makes the EliteBook," I whispered.

"But Monica Hewlett-Packard didn't sound authentic." Drew grinned.

"There are all sorts of jokes that came to mind about processing speed, and memory banks and others, but she's your sister, so I'll refrain from commenting."

"Thank you."

Drew scanned the area. "Are you sure you're okay?" he asked.

I nodded. We were silent for several seconds. Tears pooled in my eyes, and I sniffed.

"You sure?" He touched my arm gently.

A wave of guilt suddenly rushed over me for being so callous to Kathy. I hadn't had time to stop and think about the loss to Tommy and Kathy's family. A lump formed in my throat. And then anger formed. I knew I had a job to do.

"I'm okay. I need to check on Granny."

Drew nodded. "Can you make it on your own to the station?" he said, looking and sounding exasperated.

I leaned over toward him. "Yes, go, do your thing. I'll be there. I'll be happy to share everything."

"Don't go do anything foolish."

"Of course not." *Unless you call meeting a potential murderer foolish, then I'm good,* I thought.

Before I turned to join Granny on the porch, I sent a secret wink to Drew.

He looked frazzled.

I laughed lightly and pointed my finger at the crime scene.

An hour had passed, and when I returned to the boathouse to give the deputies and the ME bottles of water, I ran into Chief O'Donnell, head of the Sheriff's Department.

"Why am I not surprised to see you here?" he said.

"I was visiting Granny, and I wanted to check on the Sea Ray. And I came to the boathouse, and there she was." I pointed toward the victim.

"Mo, I have to say, between you and random joggers, I don't know who finds more dead bodies."

I looked over at the ME, a frown on my face. I twisted my mouth the way I do when I have an idea.

"Let me guess — there's more," he said.

Should I tell him what I had shared with Drew and Paige? It wasn't like it was a secret.

"She was wearing Tommy's engagement ring when I saw her yesterday."

Chief O'Donnell glanced at Kathy's hands. "And now she's not?"

"Yes, the ring is gone. And there's more."

"Of course there is."

"I found this outside on the grass. I don't know if it came from Kathy or if the wind blew it here," I lied as I handed him a piece of paper.

"What is this?" He read the title.

"It appears to be an article."

"From Jerry Ryder."

"Why would Kathy carry this with her? I mean, assuming it came from her."

"It could implicate her with the other victim." I wanted the deputies to connect the dots I already had earlier that day. The article could have come from Kathy, I was just saying.

"Ok, good job. I'll look into all of these. Thank you."

"And Chief O..."

"Yes, Molly."

"You may want to look for any drag marks on her boots. It appears she was killed somewhere else and not dragged to the boathouse from the path. See the lack of grass marks here on the wood floorboards—"

"We've got this, Molly. The question is, why would someone dump your ex-boyfriend's fiancée's body in your grandmother's boathouse?"

"It's your crime scene. So good luck."

"Can I give you a ride to the station for your statement? I know you have an alibi, but we need to know everything."

"I'll be there."

He waved me off.

"But first I have a killer to catch," I said softly under my breath.

I sent a text that read; *Can we meet? The Museum clearing. 10 pm.*

CHAPTER TWENTY-TWO

After feeding Kona and Snickers, I grabbed my backpack and filled it with a small arsenal of items I hoped I didn't need to use.

A little concerned about my meeting, I pulled my gun I called PYCA and stuck the small pistol in a holster around my bicep.

My dad had taught me how to shoot long guns at an early age, but never a pistol.

Growing up in my dad's home, we had a gun cabinet. My friends in the northeast always made fun of this. *'You have a piece of furniture dedicated to just guns?' they'd asked.*

'Don't most families?' I replied.

My PYCA was a Ruger LCP .380, a gift from my Aunt Tammera years ago. She had said it was to "protect your cute ass" and had PYCA engraved on it. I was eighteen.

I guess being the daughter of an MIA CIA operative had its benefits.

Since then, I'd upgraded to a few different PYCAs.

The few times I took PYCA with me, I stuck it in my belt and once between my boobs. My cleavage was not that ample, but it fit uncomfortably, like wearing a Victoria's Secret bra three sizes too small.

When I was in college, Aunt Tammera gave me a corset belt to carry PYCA when I went out to the campus bars. I had found that to go the restroom with it on, I had to pull it up my midriff to just below my bra line or push it down my thighs. Neither one was easy to do. Or I could take the whole darn thing off, which meant unhooking a row of eyelets. That was too time-consuming when you had to pee. Then once off, where did I put it? On the floor of the bathroom stall?

I knew I was a bit foolish concealing a gun, but I was upset. I had no intention of letting anyone ruin what I had built in this town. When I found Kathy's body, I made up mind right then and there to do whatever it took to protect my family, friends, and reputation.

Time was running out, and I knew it.

At nine-thirty, Snickers and I jumped in the golf cart and headed for the museum grounds. At this hour, there were a few cars on the street, but for the most part, the town shut down by nine o'clock.

There was a fog over the water, and the Floridian humidity left moisture in the air so thick it felt like the sky dripped condensation like a leaky faucet. The fog made the night look like an Alfred Hitchcock movie set.

After my first spring in Bay Isles, I was surprised to learn how little it rained. I had thought of Florida as one giant petri dish from all the moisture. Bay Isles was one of the sunniest cities in Florida, one of the many reasons I was happy to call it home.

When I drove by the café, the lights were off. We closed at eight. I noticed Aurora's minibike was no longer in the parking lot. So either she was released from the police station, or her dad or Todd had picked up her bike.

As I drove to the museum, I thought about Drew and his secret. When I had found out the blonde woman on Drew's boat was his sister, I was angry but relieved. Of course, I was sad and disappointed that Drew kept something so important from me, but I began to understand why.

He was trying to protect his sister. I couldn't blame him for that.

It would have been much easier if I could have stayed angry with Drew for hiding this from me. But I had more important things to do, like capture a killer.

Within fifteen minutes, I turned off the road and hit a dirt trail. I turned off the golf cart lights and used my flashlight.

The younger kids liked to come to the clearing at night to stargaze and to do the things kids weren't supposed to do, undetected by adults.

Many of the town teenagers knew about the clearing at the museum. It was surrounded by mangroves, thick trees and the water to the west, but had an ample cleared space with amazing views of the stars at night.

I hoped it was vacant except for the person I suspected murdered Jerry.

When I came to the end of the dirt trail, I parked the cart and told Snickers to stay.

I walked another hundred yards down a sandy path to the clearing. When I looked back, I couldn't see the cart with Snickers in it through the fog.

I glanced around the area, and at the far end of the clearing backing to the beach path, I saw a lone figure.

As I approached, I caught a glimpse of shiny metal clutched in their hand — a gun.

"Hello, Molly Brewster." She said like it was a common occurrence to meet in the middle of the woods.

When I got close to her, I said, "Why are you holding a gun?"

Lucy Lavender looked at me in dismay. "You can never be too sure of who or what you'll run into back here at night, all isolated."

"Can you put that away?" I asked, nodding at the gun.

"Why did you want to see me? I know you're always sticking your nose in police business," she said, ignoring my request.

"I do what's necessary to help my friends and the community," I said, still keeping an eye on the gun.

Lucy sighed. "Who knows you're here?"

"My dog," I answered honestly. I had told Granny I had a meeting, but I was sure by now she and Henrietta were fast asleep.

No reason to delay the meeting any further. "Did you kill Jerry?" I asked.

Lucy narrowed her eyes. "Why do you think I care if he's dead?" Her jaw set in a hard line. "Jerry was a piece of shit. And I'm not going to pretend I'm sorry he's dead."

I raised my eyebrows. "That's a strong sentiment coming from someone who barely knew the man. I mean, he was only here for what, a week?"

"You think you know everything."

"I know enough. I know there were three possible families he was investigating, including Aurora's dad, Kathy's brother, and your husband, Clay."

Lucy frowned, clearly not happy with my discovery.

"Lucy, Jerry Ryder wasn't here to write articles about Aurora's family or even Kathy's. He wasn't here for that. He was here because of you. Wasn't he? He had uncovered something with the help of his friends in Texas."

"What do you know?"

"When you talked to him that day in the park, he wasn't looking over at me. He was looking behind me. You asked him to meet you at the park. You were pointing out a spot toward the beach. And when he nodded, he agreed to meet you there later. Didn't he?"

Lucy let out a breath and her eyes moistened. "Come on, give me a break. I went to see him, but I never intended to hurt anyone."

"Then what happened?"

"Nothing."

"I know you've known Jerry for years. When I talked to Jerry at the police station that day, he mentioned he'd been working on a case for ten years. Yet Aurora said he just reached out to her dad recently. And Kathy's family's business with the reporter happened only a few years ago. So who would he have been following for ten years?"

Lucy sniffled and took a breath, keeping the gun pointed at my chest, but I kept talking because that's what I do. I couldn't stop.

"Ten years. Ten years. It kept rattling around in my head. Then it occurred to me that Jerry's editor said he went to Texas often over the last ten years. So I called an aunt who lives in Texas, and she found out that your husband's brother started his so-called lawn care company south of the border ten years ago.

"Lawn and Order, too. Special Grass Unit. Boy, was it a *special grass unit*. I suspect it was more than pot your family was smuggling in and delivering. And Jerry must have uncovered that your brother-in-law was involved with the Mexican Mob there."

Lucy gasped and held in a silent whimper. Her arms were visibly shaking.

"Your husband joined his brother's team and opened the same business here in Bay Isles with him ten years ago. And at first, you probably didn't know how involved your husband's business was with the smuggling. And then, as the years went by, it got bigger. And Lucy, while I know how much you love your husband, what I didn't know is that you'd be willing to do anything to help him out, including diving under boats to stash money and drugs."

Lucy laughed as she swiped at a tear on her cheek. "He was bleeding us dry. I just wanted to stop the blackmailing."

"What was he blackmailing you for?" I asked.

"You think you're so smart." She waved the gun back and forth and said, "They'll think you committed suicide for killing your boyfriend's fiancée."

Panic fluttered in my chest. Lucy intended to kill me too.

I swallowed and felt my knees wobble. I couldn't reach PYCA without a distraction.

What happened next was the distraction I needed.

CHAPTER TWENTY-THREE

There was a rustling sound from behind the bushes on the beach path. We both turned toward it.

"If you kill Mo, you're going to have to kill me too." Aurora stepped from behind the brush leading to the beach.

Aurora must have followed me.

Lucy swung around and pointed her gun at Aurora. "I have plenty of bullets. Now get over there next to Molly, where I can see you both."

Without hesitation, Aurora came over and stood next to me. My moist eyes met hers and sent a silent thank you.

"Lucy, if Mo figured it out, and I can fill in the blanks, what are you going to do when the police find out?" Aurora said, giving me a silent nod.

"The smuggling of the drugs and your cut of the money wasn't enough, was it? You were double-dipping. Getting money from both sides," I said, distracting her away from Aurora.

Lucy looked my way.

"And when Jerry Ryder found out about your side business, he threatened to expose you. That's when his blackmailing started in exchange for his silence about your company. After all, why would he tell the Mexico bad guys? You paid him off well the last ten years," I continued.

"Because Jerry was blackmailing you and demanding more and more money from you and Clay, you had to steal from the Mexico Mob," Aurora said. "But first, you had to get rid of Jerry."

"You wanted the blackmailing to end. So when you met Jerry in the park, you probably had one last boat ride with him arranged. Who would miss the sleazy reporter? Many people wanted him gone. You probably planned to tie a cannonball anchor around Jerry's legs and drop him offshore. But Kathy spoiled your plans by stabbing him first with a pie knife in a fit of outrage, so you had to act fast and figure something else out," I said, without taking my eyes off the gun.

I could tell Lucy was floundering.

She waved the gun around. "She was a bitch. Your ex-boyfriend may have been planning a life with Kathy, but I don't think he was fully aware that she was a druggie. She scouted me out the minute she got to town, wanting to make a buy."

"So you two met? At the nail salon?" This would explain Dana saying Penny wore the same polish as the new girl. Dana always mixed up Penny and Lucy. It wasn't Penny at all. It was Lucy who had met Kathy at the salon.

"Yes, I met her. She couldn't shut up about you. She thought her fiancé still had feelings for you," Lucy said.

I felt my throat close. "Is that when she told you about the reporter?"

Lucy snorted. "She told me they had met at his hotel lobby, but he wouldn't listen to her. They were yelling, and she was crying. And they were in public. She left in outrage. I could tell she hated him too. That piece of shit was going to ruin every-thing for me and so many others. And then when Jerry decided that the blackmailing wasn't enough and he wanted to break the story, I knew our relationship was over. He thought he'd win a Pulitzer Prize or something for turning us all in. I did him a favor. The mob would have tortured him before they killed him had he leaked the story."

"But you set up Kathy."

"I wanted him to be seen arguing with Kathy at the park. I told her that he wanted to meet her in the park where the bushes were behind the picnic tables, and I told her what time. She's not too smart. I told her she might want to be armed just in case. When I got there, I didn't know what to expect. At first, Kathy thought she killed him. When I came upon her bent over Jerry's crumpled body, she was crying and shaking and said she killed a man out of rage. I told her to calm down to go to my boat moored at the beach, and I would handle it," Lucy said. "She was a mess."

"So instead of helping Jerry, you finished him off. You dragged your lightweight cannonball anchor to him and clobbered him from the back side. So you could have Kathy take the fall."

"She just wouldn't shut up about it," Lucy said.

"You were worried she'd spill the beans?" Aurora said.

Lucy nodded and actually grinned when I said, "And then I handed Kathy to you on a silver platter. When you knew my past involvement with her and Tommy, and everyone knew we had been seen fighting at my café, you had to shift from your original plan. You knew Kathy would eventually be accused of murdering Jerry. She practically confessed it to Tommy the other day. What she didn't realize is that she hadn't killed him. You did."

I watched the gun quiver in her hand as I continued. "But Kathy threw a little wrench in there. Didn't she? What you didn't realize at the time is that Kathy was obsessed about not letting her hands look old. She always liked to cover them. Odd as it is, Kathy wore gloves to protect them from the sun and while driving. That day in the park, she wore driving gloves. If her fingerprints weren't on the knife, who would suspect her? That's when you buried her tennis shoe at the crime scene a day later. Wasn't it?" I said.

"She did kill him. He wasn't moving," Lucy said.

"But you had to be sure. So you clobbered Jerry on the head with the cannonball anchor your husband made," Aurora said. "The same type of anchor you use when you dive under the boats to secure the drugs and cash."

"It's lightweight enough for you to carry. And it's not hard for someone who has years of training from swimming under-water as a Weeki Wachee mermaid," I said.

Lucy waved the gun at me. "You think you know every-thing, Molly Brewster, but you don't. And it's too bad, but your deputy boyfriend will not get to hear your theory."

"But why Kathy?" I still had to hear Lucy admit to killing Kathy.

"She ruined everything," Lucy murmured. "I had my black-mail payoff with me, and she took it."

"Who took it?" I asked.

"Kathy! She found it in the boat while I was —"

"—while you were finishing Jerry off and making sure he didn't talk?" I said.

"She must have hidden the money down her boots. Because after I dropped her off, I noticed it was gone. Clay was so upset with me. He wanted me to find it. I went to her hotel, and it was so easy getting a maid to let me in."

"Did you get the blood money back?" I asked.

Lucy floundered, but kept talking.

"She had trashed the room. She's not much of a house-keeper. I thought I was messy. Kathy managed to make the hotel suite she'd been in for a few days look like she hosted a bachelorette party there for a week. Clothes, shoes, and makeup on every surface. But no money." Lucy lifted the gun higher.

"Is that when you stole her tennis shoe?"

"That sounds about right. At first, I wasn't sure what I'd do with it." Lucy became more animated. "That's when I decided I'd confront her about the money."

I frowned. "But why did you take my dog leash?"

"See, I knew how smart you were last year in solving that fisherman's murder. So I got worried. I went to your apartment to talk to you, and you were gone. I went out back and found your paddleboard. And when I saw your makeshift anchor with the dog leash and weight, I knew it was only a matter of time before you figured out how I use a makeshift anchor with a cannonball." Lucy's jaw clenched, and I could tell she was getting angrier. "Clay made the special anchors for me because I can dive under the boats. And they don't leave anchor marks."

"So Clay knew about Jerry?"

"Oh he knew about the blackmailing. He's the muscle of the LAO operation, and I'm the brains. He helped take care of any issues."

"That requires muscle. I get it." My mind was cataloging everything. And I thought about her last comment. If Clay was the muscle and she was the brains, then I wondered if I caught her off guard, if I could take her before she got a shot off. I had a secret weapon. I could whistle for Snickers.

"What's your plan to get out of this one? To close the loop? What was your story going to be, Lucy?" I asked. "You used me as your fall guy. You tried to pin Kathy's murder on me. I'm sure you hid her engagement ring somewhere in my café or apartment. And how did you get her body in Granny's boathouse? I know you killed her at the LAO offices. I saw all the Kapok tree trimmings and smooshed flowers there when I went by this afternoon. I also found several of the cannonball anchors."

Lucy looked at me, eyes wide. "You do one thing, and you don't think. It's not like I had this master plan. The Mexico business partners started stealing the boats because they were looking for something. They're on to Clay, and they're looking for the missing drugs. We had a special cubby installed under our Sea Ray. We just got in too deep."

"And Jerry knew?" I said.

"Yes. He wanted more and more money. And when the money wasn't enough, he wanted the story. I needed him out of the picture. With him gone, we could pay the Mexican Mafia back."

"You killed two people," I said.

"Two terrible people," she said.

I shook my head and took a step closer to her.

"Why did you have to stick your nose in this? You couldn't leave it alone," Lucy said.

"Lucy, it doesn't have to be this way."

"You know this isn't going to end well for you, Molly Brewster. Too many people are dead already," Lucy said.

"Let's stop the charades. And you need to come clean. No one else needs to get hurt."

"This side business we have going on is just too lucrative to give up," Lucy said.

"You killed Jerry and then Kathy over money?"

"Everything has a price." Lucy raised her gun at me. Her eyes were brimming with tears, and her hand was shaking as she held the gun out.

Aurora took one step toward Lucy.

Lucy swung the gun off me and pointed it at Aurora. "Stay where you are."

All of a sudden, with an amazing amount of agility and speed, Granny, clutching her cane, and Henrietta, clutching her handbag, came rushing into the clearing. As soon as Granny caught sight of the gun in Lucy's hands, she bent over and clasped her heart.

Granny looked at Lucy and lifted her cane and pointed it at her. "What — the hell — is going on here?" she asked, between deep breaths.

"Oh my God," Lucy said. "Who are all these people?"

"Your worst nightmare," Granny said when she got another breath.

Lucy pointed at me. "If these are your friends, tell them to stop, or I'll shoot you."

I had a big lump in my throat when I thought about the people who would risk their lives for me.

I quietly said, "Calm down, everyone. We can figure this out."

I secretly winked at Aurora and let out a low whistle. Lucy's eyes widened like I'd lost my mind.

I silently counted to ten. When Lucy turned to see the chocolate streak burst into the clearing, I delivered a kick to her face, knocking her off-balance. The gun flew out of her hand. Aurora kicked it out of the way as Lucy managed to flip over and elbowed me in the ribs. I screamed.

Snickers pounced on her, snarling and snapping. He had hold of Lucy's arm while Granny was smacking her over the head with the cane. Henrietta used an aerosol can of what looked and smelled like hairspray from her handbag to spray at Lucy. I figured Henrietta thought it was mace, or she didn't like Lucy's hairstyle.

What a mess.

That's when I caught a glimpse of Drew and Deputy Cross running over to us.

Deputy Cross hesitated, looking at the scene as if he was trying to figure out who the bad guy was.

Drew pulled a pair of handcuffs out of his belt and knelt and heaved Lucy up.

"Unhand me!" Lucy yelled.

"I'll try, but I don't think they'll come off." Drew winked. "Let's try these bracelets on."

Drew handcuffed Lucy.

I turned to Drew, once Deputy Cross escorted Lucy away. "But how'd you know we were here?"

"A concerned citizen called us and said they'd witnessed a scrambling of odd vehicles at the park area that was usually closed at this hour."

"Odd?" I bit my lower lip.

"I suppose you and Snickers drove the golf cart, Aurora drove the minibike and Granny, well there's a bright red Gatsby-looking Model T retro scooter tethered on the curb with its two front wheels in the grass, and there's a bright pink electric bike with a flagpole flying an American flag. That probably belongs to Henrietta."

"And what was odd about that? This is Bay Isles, after all. That would hardly warrant a call to the police station. It must have been a tourist," I said.

Granny hugged me. "I took the bike. You said you had a meeting in the clearing."

"I did?" I said.

"You did. You were mumbling and pulling on your new haircut. I don't think you were thinking straight when you left my house. I was worried about you," Granny said.

"So Granny called me," Aurora said, and walked over and gave me a big hug. She released me and stepped back. "Granny told me all about the evening. Mo, I'm so sorry. I know how you feel. I went to the café and your apartment. When I didn't find you, I called Granny back, and she remembered your meeting. I jumped on my minibike and came here."

Granny looked at Drew. "I wanted to help too, so I took my old electric bike. But Aurora beat me here," Granny said.

"Granny, you shouldn't be riding a bike, electric or not, at night, on a dirt road that is old as you are," I said.

Granny scratched her bony middle finger on her nose and winked.

I turned to Henrietta. And she shrugged her shoulders and said, "You right, Ms. Mo. Granny hasn't ridden a bike in the dark in years. I follow behind her in the electric scoot thing." She made a gesture with her hands like she was revving a motorcycle. "It's very quiet."

"All right, all right, ladies, I should be asking what in God's name are you all doing at the park at this hour?" Drew said to my three accomplices and me. Snickers was sitting at my heels. "And not discussing *how* you got here, but *why* you are here. And *why* Lucy Lavender had a gun."

Drew fixed his gaze on me.

"I had a hunch about who killed Jerry," I said. "And checking it out at night was more secretive as far as the being-seen-in-public angle was concerned."

"So you invited a potential murderer to the park at night without a thought to call the police?"

Granny sucked in her breath, and Henrietta looked down at her shoes.

"If I called the police every time I interviewed a suspect, you'd have me arrested."

Drew stared. "So I'm supposed to believe Lucy was just planning a stroll at the museum park clearing after ten, and you ran into her and decided to interview her?"

"No," I said. "I did text her to meet me, here like Granny said."

Drew narrowed his eyes and gave me and then Granny an exasperated look. "Can you give my deputies and me a few minutes to secure the scene, and then will you all please meet me at the station?"

"Ok," I said. "But—"

"No buts" he said.

"But I don't care for the coffee at the station," I said. "If you let me run by the café to get us all *good* coffee, then we can meet at the police station, and we'll fill you in."

"Last I checked, you were headed to the station," Drew sighed.

I frowned.

Drew turned to Aurora. "Aurora, you can go and bring us some coffees and," Drew paused and turned toward Granny and Henrietta, "I'll be expecting all of you in for statements."

Henrietta looked pleased, like it was an honor to be asked to give a testimony.

Drew turned to Aurora. "I don't suppose you can grab some of those chocolate pudding cookies too. I managed to miss lunch and dinner today."

"No need," Henrietta said. "I made two lasagnas, a casserole, four dozen cookies, and two Bundt cakes today."

We all stared at her.

"Sorry, I cook when I'm nervous. And having a dead person in our boat garage and all those police people around made me nervous."

Drew rubbed his jaw and said, "I guess it couldn't hurt to bring the food too."

Granny turned on a flashlight, and the three ladies walked toward the path to the trail. I heard Henrietta say, "Oh boy, it's like a dinner party."

Drew turned to me and held me in his arms, and we kissed.

"Molly Brewster, what am I going to do with you?"

CHAPTER TWENTY-FOUR

I t took a couple of days for the deputies to untangle everything. But in the end, Lucy and her husband Clay were behind bars. If Kathy were still alive, she would be facing attempted manslaughter charges.

Aurora and Penny were off the hook. Tommy was heartbroken. And Granny and Henrietta were thrilled to be a part of the arrest.

Chief O'Donnell and Ranger Paige Powell had flown to Texas. They had assisted the DEA when they captured LAO's primary contact in Mexico. They were arriving back in Florida to face charges with the rest of the drug smuggling crew. Due to the notoriety of the reporter, Jerry Ryder Mistack, the entire takedown and blackmailing had made national news.

And best of all, I helped Drew solve the case.

I stood on my café's front porch saying goodbye to Tommy. "Do you promise to keep in touch?"

Tommy nodded. "I still can't believe I'm going back without her. I was so shocked that she was murdered, I completely blocked out of my mind the trouble she had caused."

I touched his arm softly. "But the perpetrator is behind bars, and that should make you rest easier."

"Thanks to you and your crew," Tommy said, as a lone tear slipped out of his right eye and ran down his tanned cheek. Tommy didn't wipe it off, and it seemed as if he hadn't even realized the tear had escaped.

I smiled and said softly, "If it's any consolation, Lucy will go away for a long time for what she did, even if she did claim self-defense."

He nodded and gave me a big hug. His lower lip quivered as he turned to leave.

"I'll call you," Tommy said, as he got into the taxi. "And Mo, I left some boxes at the hotel. Kathy had done some major shopping. There are online shipments coming to you as well. I told the hotel to forward everything to you. Please donate it, keep it, or return it. I can't deal with any of that right now."

I nodded and stood on the porch until the taxi was out of sight.

I returned to the café and sat next to Aurora.

Granny Dee, Henrietta, Aurora, and I were sitting at a round table.

I whispered to Aurora, "Are you doing okay now?"

Aurora had her hair pulled back and secured with a tortoise-shell comb. I was pleased to see all the rhinestones were intact. That's one piece of evidence I had miscalculated. I had a second thought. The missing rhinestone may have belonged to Kathy.

Aurora nodded. "I'm doing fine. But I might as well tell you all that I had hired Amelia, Todd's sister, to be my dad's legal counsel in the case about the defective dental products."

I squeezed Aurora's arm. That would explain why I had seen Aurora giving Amelia cash at the park that day. I had all sorts of thoughts about the exchange I had seen, and I wanted to approach Aurora, but it was an impossible situation with too many variables. It would have been unfair to corner Aurora on the subject, and I knew in time she would let me know what was going on.

"That's great, sweetie. I know Amelia and her uncle are good lawyers. They'll help your family resolve this quickly," Granny said.

"I have to trust Amelia. She can be a pain sometimes, but it is a small comfort that she is related to my boyfriend. I'll take any help I can get," Aurora said.

"Mo, before you sat down, I was questioning Aurora about some of the facts. And she was saying that Christine said the ME confirmed that the stab wound to Jerry had come from a left-handed person, indicating Kathy. After the loss of blood weakened him, Lucy stepped in. And in Lucy's testimony, she claimed she hadn't wanted Jerry to bring attention to himself by thrashing around in the bushes of a crowded park," Granny said.

"So, she whacked him?" Henrietta asked.

"Most likely to prevent the risk of the stab wound not killing him, or maybe she was afraid help would arrive quickly enough to save his life," Aurora said.

"When the victim collapsed, the killer stepped behind him and clobbered him on the left side of the head," I said.

"Oh my," Granny said. "After he was stabbed, was that when he grabbed Kathy? Didn't Christine say there were pink fibers under his nails?"

"Maybe," I said. "But we'll know for sure when the ME tests Kathy's skirt that Tom gave the detectives. I do know one thing: My good friend here, Aurora, has never worn pink in her life." I smiled.

"You got that right," Aurora said and winked at me.

"Since the right side of the back of the head was unaffected, this indicated that the killer was most likely right-handed. My guess is Lucy told Kathy to get in her boat, then she had planned to weight the body with an anchor and dump him offshore somewhere," I said.

"She's been caught up in all the drug money, and I think she's been teetering on the brink of sanity and what's right or wrong for a while," said Granny softly. "When Kathy threatened to tell what happened with Jerry, it pushed Lucy farther over the edge. And her decision to strangle Kathy and blame it on Mo wasn't even rational. She wanted to keep the money train coming, and to do that she had to keep the secret."

"Lucy couldn't let Jerry, or anyone discover their money and drug trafficking," Aurora said.

"Once they started stealing from the Mexican mob, their contacts were trying to figure out their con," I said.

"So, the mob started to steal the boats," Aurora said. "To find the money or drugs or how they did it?"

"They used the LAO logbook for all their drop locations," I said. "Once the mob went after them, they couldn't go to the police, or it would have blown their gig."

"Don't they watch TV? You don't screw the mob. It could have ended a lot worse. They wouldn't be in jail. They could have been buried in a ditch," Aurora said.

"Or wearing cement boots at the bottom of the Gulf of Mexico," Granny said.

"How did it go so crazy?" Henrietta asked.

"Guilt," I said. "I think Kathy was having a hard time with the fact that she thought she killed Jerry, and Lucy helped her cover it up. She had told Tom that she wanted to tell him something. Kathy was acting strange since the festival and exhibiting signs of manic depression. Tom said she was drinking more than usual and forgetting stuff."

"Do you think Kathy wanted to confess?"

"I think Lucy wanted the deputies to discover Kathy's white tennis shoe at the park. But instead, Snickers found it. Lucy was trying to push the deputies to the conclusion that Kathy was the murderer."

"But wouldn't that also point to Lucy as an accomplice?" Granny said.

"I'm sure she would have lied. Or maybe her plan all along was to kill Kathy too. So there were no loose ends," I said.

"Lucy wanted to pin Jerry's death on Kathy, and then planned to get rid of Kathy by pinning her death on you?" Granny said. "That's twisted. She had to be working with that Mexican mob for so long, she couldn't tell right from wrong anymore and got way over her head."

"What made you think it wasn't just Kathy as the murderer?" Aurora asked.

"I saw a paper with an article about LAO in Kathy's purse, along with her driving gloves. And I kept thinking of all the people Jerry had pissed off. He made it easy for so many to have a motive. Ruined lives. Destroyed businesses. And I assume Lucy wasn't the only one Jerry blackmailed. I thought about the Agatha Christie novel, *Murder on the Orient Express,* and how so many people wanted the victim dead that they all contributed to the murder," I said.

"Makes sense," Granny said. "You're a natural sleuth, Mo."

"What about Penny's toenail polish matching Kathy's? That's still a mystery," Henrietta said.

"No, it's not," I said. "Penny told me she had seen Lucy wearing that color, so Penny went to the salon and had it applied too."

"Oh," Granny and Henrietta both said.

"I talked to Dana at the salon, and she said she threw out the color *Get Cherried Away* because those three women were the only ones ever to wear it. And two out of three hadn't ended well."

Everyone laughed.

"Try this," I said, handing Aurora one of the blueberry muffins I'd baked for Easter.

"Gladly." Aurora took a large bite and a blissful expression spread over her face. But then it suddenly turned to horror.

"Ew!" Aurora screamed as she spit a mouthful of muffin into a napkin.

"Sorry, that bad, huh?" I asked.

Aurora's face lit up with acknowledgement. "I love your baking, Mo, but the extra ingredient isn't necessary." She opened her paper napkin and a diamond ring caked with blueberries, sparkled from the clump of unchewed muffin.

I flushed with embarrassment. "I'm so sorry. That must have been hidden in the flour bin when I made muffins this morning. I was preoccupied with my thoughts when I mechanically baked six dozen muffins. I must have missed it."

Granny and Henrietta leaned over the clump of muffin.

"Aha!" Henrietta exclaimed.

"Brilliant!" Granny said. "Hey, I heard that in some countries finding a ring in a baked good means you're the next to get engaged." She chuckled.

Aurora's eyes widened, and she pushed the napkin and ring toward my coffee cup. "Not me!"

I gave them a sour look, then eyed the ring. "Yup, it looks to be Kathy's engagement ring that Deputy Drew has been looking for."

"I wonder how Lucy snuck in our kitchen to plant evidence?" Aurora asked.

I shrugged. "There are many nooks and crannies in this place," I said, "but Lucy probably couldn't risk a customer finding it. She probably wanted the police to find it."

"A pathetic attempt to pin evidence on you," Aurora said. "Speaking of that, did you ever give the tennis shoe to Drew?" Aurora asked.

Suddenly I heard Drew's voice, low and gentle, behind me. "Did I just hear something about you finding a piece of evidence in an active crime scene?"

He startled me. "Oh right, sorry. I meant to give it to you. Snickers dug it up. But when I went back to my paddleboard, it was gone. I figured Lucy stole the shoe when she took my leash to strangle Kathy."

His light blue eyes narrowed, and he never stopped watching me. Deputy Drew looked like he finally had a chance to get eight hours of sleep. He looked relaxed and sexy.

"Do you want a sandwich? We have a freshly baked ham for the party tomorrow," I asked Drew.

He leaned over to give me a quick kiss and nodded. "That would be great. I skipped breakfast, and I'm starving."

I nodded.

"Hello ladies. How are you all today? Are you ready for Easter Sunday tomorrow?" Drew pulled out a chair and sat where I had been sitting.

They all started talking at once.

I smiled as I walked into the café kitchen to make Drew's sandwich. I was lucky to have a home that was filled with friends and family. Their love and support made me feel so welcome in the community, and I was so blessed. And I was double blessed to have my loving pets and a boyfriend.

————

I was finishing the small plate of food when I heard Drew say, "Excuse me, ladies."

He slipped into the tiny kitchen. He pulled me into his arms and hugged me so hard it hurt. I'd been half worried he might have been mad at me after I'd overstepped my boundaries in the investigation. But his passionate kiss told me he wasn't holding any grudges.

"I've been thinking. I could have lost you when Lucy pulled a gun on you. Promise next time you'll call me before trying to capture a murderer."

"Ok, I promise," I said, hoping I never had to break that oath.

"Are your fingers crossed?" Drew asked as I felt a tug at my right arm.

I showed him my hand, feeling relived that my left wrist felt so much better.

Drew held my right hand. "Mo, this last week had me thinking a lot. And I'm sure having your ex-boyfriend and ex-best friend show up and then announcing their engagement made you wonder about the future. I know it got me thinking about our relationship." Drew paused.

My heart skipped a beat as my gaze met his blue eyes.

"And I have a question to ask you," he said softly.

There were plenty of questions that ran through my mind. But one that I wasn't sure I was prepared for.

For the first time in my life, I had a long list of friends who cared about me, and I had family close by, not to mention a community of interesting people, a career I loved, and my boyfriend standing in front of me who made my heart flutter. What else could I want? Was I ready for his question?

I grinned at Drew and waited for the question.

———

Will Deputy Drew Powell ask Molly to marry him? What new mystery will Molly and her friends have to solve? Find out in the next Holidays are Murder series book: *The Fourth Murder*.

RECIPE COFFEE BREAK

STRAWBERRY PIE*

GRANNY'S NOTE: DO NOT USE A SERRATED KNIFE TO CUT THE
PIE. (KIDDING)

*T*he same recipe that won the Palma County baking contest. Mary Dedham suggests you use store-bought Florida berries.

For one 10-inch Pie

- Juice: 1 Pint fresh strawberries & 2 cups water
- Pie: 2 Cups strawberry juice
- 2 Cups sugar
- 1/3 Cup strawberry gelatin
- 3 Tablespoons Cornstarch
- 1 Baked 10-inch single crust (store-bought or make your own)
- 1 ½ Quarts strawberries (stems removed, washed & drained)
- 2 Cups Fresh Whipped Cream

1. First make the juice: Cook in stainless steel saucepan over medium heat until berries are pale (about 5 minutes). Strain and reserve the juice.

2. To make the Pie: Combine the strawberry juice and the sugar, and boil for a couple of minutes until the sugar is dissolved completely.

3. Add the gelatin and stir until it boils. Dissolve the cornstarch in a little cold water, add quickly to above mixture and cook, stirring slowly until a clear bubble forms (about 5 minutes). Cool until it's as thick as molasses.

4. Pour just enough juice into the baked pie crust to cover the bottom.

5. Arrange the berries over the crust. (Cut the berries in half). Pour on remaining juice, making sure to cover the berries completely.

6. Refrigerate and when ready to serve, top with fresh whipped cream. Mary Dedham used Easter-themed sprinkles across the whipped cream to add color.

HENRIETTA'S HAM LOAF

WHEN HENRIETTA GREW UP NO FOOD WENT TO WASTE. SHE
LEARNED TO MAKE HAM BALLS & HAM LOAF FROM THE
LEFTOVER PORK ROAST AND HAM BUTT. GRIND THE MEAT
USING A MEDIUM BLADE FROM OF THE MEAT GRINDER (OR
FOOD CHOPPER).

- 1 ½ pounds ground ham
- ¾ pound fresh pork
- 2 eggs, beaten
- 1 ½ Cups breadcrumbs
- 1 Cup Milk
- Salt & pepper to taste
- ¾ Cup packed brown sugar
- 2 Tablespoons flour
- 1 Tablespoon dry mustard
- 1 Tablespoon vinegar

1. Preheat the oven to 325° F. In a large bowl, put the ham and pork. In a smaller bowl, put the eggs. Add the breadcrumbs to the eggs and allow them to soak.
2. Dump the milk and the crumbs into the meat bowl, add salt and pepper and mix well. Place in buttered bread pan.
3. Mix the brown sugar, flour, dry mustard and vinegar

together in a small bowl and spread on top the loaf.
Bake for1 1 ½ hours, until the meat shrinks away
from the edge of the pan.

4. Serve and enjoy!

AURORA'S BLUEBERRY MUFFINS

START YOUR DAY WITH A SMILE WITH THESE PERFECT
MUFFINS. AURORA SAYS TO KEEP THE MUFFINS FROM HAVING
PURPLE BLOBS OR PATCHES, LAYER THE BERRIES INTO THE
MUFFIN CUPS INSTEAD OF STIRRING THEM INTO THE BATTER.

- 6 Tablespoon salted butter, melted and cooled
- 1 teaspoon vanilla extract
- 2 eggs
- 1/3 Cup whole milk
- ¾ cup sugar
- 1 1/3 cup all-purpose flour
- 1 ½ teaspoon baking powder
- ½ teaspoon salt
- 2 cups blueberries (fresh or frozen or mix) (& don't worry about thawing the frozen ones)
- 1 batch basic streusel (recipe follows)

Makes 1 dozen or 6 Jumbo Muffins

P reheat oven to 350 degrees. Line 12 (regular) or 6 (jumbo) muffin pan with paper liners.

1. In large bowl, whisk together the melted butter and eggs. Add milk and vanilla and whisk until well combined.

2. In a separate bowl, whisk together flour, sugar, baking powder and salt.

3. Add flour mixture to butter mixture and carefully fold together with rubber spatula until just combined. (Do not over mix or muffins will be tough.) Aurora's hint: the batter should still have a few streaks of flour.

4. Spoon about 1 Tbsp of batter (or 2 Tbsp for jumbo muffins) into each prepared muffin well. Using half the berries, sprinkle the batter in each well with an equal amount of berries. Using half of the remaining batter, top the berries with an equal amount of batter. Sprinkle the remaining berries as before and top each well with an equal amount of remaining batter. Mound the streusel evenly over the top of each filled well.

5. Bake until the tops are golden brown, and a muffin bounces back when you poke it gently in the center with a finger, 22-26 minutes for standard size and 30-35 minutes for the jumbo.

6. For basic streusel topping- In a bowl of the food processor, pulse 1/3 cup flour and 3 ½ Tbsp firmly packed brown sugar once or twice till mixed. Cut in 2 ½ Tbsp cold, salted butter, cut into ½ inch pieces using 1-second pulses until streusel just starts to clump together and visible butter chunks are no bigger than pea-size. (If you don't have a processor, you can combine butter, flour and brown sugar in a bowl and use two knives or rub between your fingers to break up into pea-size pieces.) The streusel should be a mixture of crumbly and chunky. Can be stored in refrigerator for up to 2 weeks in a sealed container.

Henrietta's variation on Aurora's blueberry muffins. She uses lemons from Granny's garden.

Blueberry—lemon: Use 2 cups blueberries and add 2 tsp lemon extract and 1 Tbsp lemon zest to butter mixture.

MOLLY'S EASY HONEY GLAZED HAM

SINCE THERE ARE NO HONEY BAKED HAM STORES IN BAY
ISLES, MO PREFERS A QUICK VERSION OF THE POPULAR
EASTER HAM

- 4 lb ham, boneless, fully cooked
- 1 can Lemon-lime soda
- 12 oz. Honey
- ½ teaspoon Mustard
- ½ teaspoon Cloves, ground
- ¼ teaspoon Cinnamon, ground

1. Place ham and lemon-lime soda into crockpot.
2. If your pot has a rack, you can use it. Cover and cook on low 6 to 8 hours (high 3-4 hours). Thirty minutes before serving, combine honey, mustard, cloves and cinnamon and 3 tablespoons from bottom of crock pot. Spread glaze over ham and continue cooking.
3. Let ham stand for 15 minutes before serving.

Makes 1 ham - 12 Servings

HEARTY CHEESE BALL APPETIZER
(ALMOST KETO!)

Can be made up to several days ahead.
Makes 1 large or 2 Small Balls

- 8 oz. cream cheese
- ½ cup sour cream
- 2 Cups shredded Swiss cheese, room temperature
- 2 Cups shredded Cheddar cheese, room temperature
- ½ Cup finely chopped onion
- 1 jar pimiento (2 oz.), in its juice, chopped
- 10 slices of bacon, crisp cooked, drained, crumbled
- 2 Tablespoons dill pickle relish
- ½ Cup finely chopped pecans, divided
- ¼ Cup snipped parsley
- 1 Tablespoon poppy seeds
- Salt & Pepper to taste

1. In large bowl beat together cream cheese and sour cream until fluffy.

2. Beat in Swiss cheese, cheddar cheese, onion, undrained pimiento, pickle relish, half the bacon, ¼ cup pecans, dash of salt and pepper.
3. Cover and chill until firm.
4. On wax paper, shape into one large ball or two smaller balls.
5. In a small bowl combine remaining bacon, remaining pecans, parsley and poppy seeds.
6. Pour mixture onto a clean sheet of wax paper.
7. Roll cheese balls in seed mixture to coat, taking up mixture; wrap and chill.
8. Let stand 30 minutes at room temperature before serving. When ready to serve place on serving dish with crackers or veggies on the side.

ABOUT THE AUTHOR

PAM MOLL

Pam Moll loves traveling and attributes her creative inspiration to it. Many of her adventures are to remote tropical islands. She lives on an island near Saint Petersburg, Florida. Pam has published numerous novels, calendars, and guidebooks.

I hope you enjoyed Book Two of the Molly Brewster Mystery Series! Your feedback is important to me and inspires me.

If you liked Book Two: *Boats, Bunnies and Bodies,* please go to www.gopamela.com and register to be the first to receive Book 3 in the series: *Apple Pie a la Murder and I Scream.* Get on the list to Pre-Order Book 3 and 4 and win an Amazon Gift Card: www.gopamela.com

In the meantime, if you liked this and other stories by Pam, please go to where you bought it and write a review, so other readers can hear from you.

Or leave a review on Goodreads or Amazon. Thanks for reading!

Please provide a positive review by clicking here:

My Book

PEPPERMINT MOCHA MURDER

Click here to BUY: https://gopamela.com/peppermint-mocha-murder/

To save the season, you'll have to catch a culinary killer.

Molly Brewster's new café bookshop is the go-to spot for strong coffee, flaky pastries, and juicy gossip. But everything changes when the tide drags in a dead body, practically on the shop's doorstep. As a newcomer to the tight-knit South Florida village, Molly is pegged by the County Sheriff as the prime suspect.

Determined to track down the real killer to clear her name, Molly enlists the help of her loyal chocolate Lab, her cantankerous Granny Dee, and the handsome Deputy Lucky. With Holly Fest just days away, she must rely on her wits and her fiery spirit to crack the case. Molly's holiday season is about to go from hectic to downright dangerous.

Peppermint Mocha Murder is the lighthearted book in the Molly Brewster Mystery series, a set of cozy murder mysteries. If you like mouthwatering recipes, charming island villages, and twists you won't see coming, then you'll love Agatha Lane's delectable whodunnit.

Buy *Peppermint Mocha Murder* to read a funny mystery for festive foodies today!

ISLAND OF LIES

Click here to BUY: http://bit.ly/IslandofLiesBook1

Two survivors. One island. No one to trust...

Ryleigh Lane desperately needs a vacation. The whistle-blower is about to appear in court to go up against a corrupt pharmaceutical exec. If she's successful, the case will reveal a deadly secret. Shortly before the trial, a carefree cruise with her new boyfriend, Elliot, changes everything. A sudden storm leaves them stranded alone on a tiny island.

Island of Lies is the first book in the Survival Island series, a set of suspenseful thriller novels. If you like sizzling chemistry, riveting suspense, and twists you won't see coming, then you'll love Pam Moll's captivating series starter.

Buy *Island of Lies* to journey to the island today!

GIRL ALONE ON AN ISLAND

CLICK HERE TO BUY : HTTP://BIT.LY/GIRLALONEONANISLAND

Click here to BUY : http://bit.ly/GirlaloneonanIsland

A deadly paradise. A family secret. Fighting for her life could mean saving thousands more...

Girl Alone on an Island is the second book in the exhilarating Survival Island series. If you like fast-paced action, gripping suspense, and captivating plot twists, then you'll love Pam Moll's nail-biting novel.

DIAMOND ISLAND LIES

Click here to BUY:
http://bit.ly/DiamondIslandOrderNow

A forgotten treasure. An ill-fated island. Twin sisters are hot on the trail of a multi-generational mystery…

Diamond Island is the third book in the Survival Island saga, a series of sea adventure novels that mix the action of Clive Cussler with the romance of Nora Roberts. If you like vivid tropical settings, pulse-pounding plot twists, and passion on the high seas, then you'll love Pamela Laux Moll's steamy thrillers.

Buy *Diamond Island* to return to a dangerous paradise today!